# CAN YOU PROMISE ME SPRING ?

## ALISON LOHANS

Cover by
Rick Ormand

Scholastic Canada Ltd.

**Scholastic Canada Ltd.**
123 Newkirk Road, Richmond Hill, Ontario, Canada
L4C 3G5

**Scholastic Inc.**
730 Broadway, New York, NY 10003, USA

**Ashton Scholastic Limited**
Private Bag 1, Penrose, Auckland, New Zealand

**Ashton Scholastic Pty Limited**
PO Box 579, Gosford, NSW 2250, Australia

**Scholastic Publications Ltd.**
Holly Walk, Leamington Spa, Warwickshire CV32 4LS,
England

**Canadian Cataloguing in Publication Data**

Lohans, Alison, 1949-
    Can you promise me spring?

ISBN 0-590-74008-3

I. Title.

PS8573.053C3 1991      jC813'.54      C91-093917-9
PZ7.L65Ca  1991

6 5 4 3 2          Printed in Canada          1 2 3 4 5/9

*In loving memory of Michael
whose long, courageous battle will never be forgotten
by those who knew him.*

# Contents

# 1
# Fall

I was out running with Heather the day I finally realized something was wrong with Jamie.

It was early October, one of those crisp golden afternoons that makes a person feel ecstatic just to be alive. The clean prairie air was nippy enough to chase some people into bulky sweaters or even jackets and gloves. But Heather and I were in our jogging suits, and the blood pumping through me pushed away any traces of cold.

"Wait up!" Heather puffed. "Lori Carmichael, you're disgusting! Can't you even *pretend* to be tired?"

I didn't want to stop. The top of the creek dike was fantastic for running, and I wanted to go at least as far as the huge willow by the footbridge. But I turned and jogged backwards instead. Heather Graham's face was pink from exertion and her chunky body was chugging along like a locomotive about to run out of steam. "Stop here if you want," I said. "I'm going on to the tree."

1

"Show-off," she muttered, and straightened her glasses. But then she grinned and waved me on.

I took off with long springy strides that lengthened until I was running on my toes. My legs felt warm and elastic and strong, and the wind rushing past me, streaming my hair out behind me, blew away all thoughts. It was as if my body had taken full control, with my mind only coming along to enjoy the ride. It basked in sunlight sparkling off the band of blue water, in gleaming clumps of willows wearing their autumn gold. Out of the corner of my eye I saw squabbling Canada geese flying northwest in a ragged V formation.

And then I'd reached the willow. Its trunk rose up in separate columns, forming a small hollow at the base where kids hid secret notes and treasures. My fingers fleetingly touched the grey crinkled bark, then I turned to go back.

Heather was running to meet me. "Your brother just fell down!"

"What?" I stopped and looked across Wascana Creek, following her pointing finger.

On the opposite side my kid brother was getting to his feet, while his friend John Duncan waited. Ever since he'd turned twelve Jamie had been stretching out into a network of gangly arms and legs, and his co-ordination had vanished. But lately he seemed to be tripping and falling too often — and besides, he should have been back on his feet sooner.

"Hey, Jamie!" I yelled. "Co-ordination!"

He looked at me and swung his arms in a gesture of disgust.

"What'd you trip on, your shadow?" John's kidding voice floated over to me.

I grinned at Heather. "Think he needs his big sister to help him up?" But a twinge of genuine concern nipped at me as I ran across the footbridge.

Jamie's face was red with frustration when I reached him. "Stupid idiot legs," he was muttering. His mouse-brown hair swung into his eyes momentarily.

"What's the matter?" Heather had caught up with me.

Jamie slapped his thighs. "My dumb legs're half asleep. All pins and needles. How'm I supposed to keep my balance?" He coughed the short hacking cough that had been with him for a while.

I looked more closely at him. Jamie was all skin and bones, probably because of the growing he'd been doing. But I thought something didn't seem quite right, maybe because recently he'd been walking with a wobbly, unsure gait.

John Duncan peered at me through his thick glasses. "You girls out for a run?"

Heather groaned. "Lori is. For me it's torture."

I shot her a wicked grin. "You said you wanted to lose weight. Ready?" I backed off, jogging again.

"Lori! Can't you even let me catch my breath?"

3

So I waited, wishing the boys would go. My kid brother could be impossible, especially when he got together with John — which was often, since the Duncans lived right across the street. Why John, who was fourteen, chose to hang around with my twelve-year-old brother, didn't make sense to me. Except that John was one of those shy smart kids who hide behind thick lenses — and since Jamie sometimes was too brilliant for his own good, the two of them spent hours building motors and other gadgets.

"C'mon, Duncan," Jamie said impatiently. "I want to look through my new *Edmunds Scientific Catalogue*." Absently he began scratching his neck.

I glanced at Heather. "Would you believe I'm related to a monkey? He's scratching his fleas again."

"Shut up, buffalo face," Jamie growled.

Heather giggled. "*Buffalo* face?"

"It's buffalo everything with these two," I said.

John brushed his hair back from his forehead. "Okay, J.C., we'll go look at your catalogue. But no more tripping or I'll call the ambulance."

Jamie made an obscene gesture and started down the dike. And then he slipped.

The breath went out of me in a startled whoosh.

John's stocky form moved quickly. "What's with you, Carmichael?"

"Get lost," Jamie muttered.

Unexpected worry nibbled at me. Grabbing my kid brother's arm to help him up, I looked him in the eye. "Are you sick or something?"

Jamie jerked away. "Don't you dare say anything to Mom," he threatened hoarsely. "Think I want to get dragged off to Doc Olsen's again?"

I'd forgotten about Jamie's visits to the doctor. My life was so busy, Jamie usually got lost in the clutter. I hardly even saw him, except at mealtimes.

He scowled at me. "You'll be sorry."

I grinned. Jamie's type of revenge was nothing short of genius. Mom had been the most recent target. She'd been on his case for months, nagging at him to keep his bed made — until the day she found it that way, neatly glued at the corners with super glue and impossible to unmake. She just about hit the ceiling, so Jamie finally relented and undid his work with a bottle of acetone. Mom hadn't bugged him about his bed since.

Heather giggled. "Lori knows better." Most of my friends had heard about Jamie's feats.

"I thought so," Jamie said gruffly. Carefully he worked his way to level ground.

I sat down and picked a dried head of wild oats. A pair of mallards swam on the calm water, trailing behind them two sets of silver-edged ripples. Not far away a fish jumped with a little *plop*. Concentric circles widened across the surface until they touched the far bank and broke. The ducks silently veered in their course.

Heather sighed and nudged up her glasses. "Beautiful."

"Yeah." I chewed the weed stalk. Derek had said something about coming over to compare notes for chemistry. Our lab books were due, and because chemistry was easier for me, Derek often asked for help. $AgNO_3$. I looked at the tiny black spots on my hands. I'd been extra careful in lab, but even so silver nitrate had spattered onto me. Heather had a larger splotch on her wrist.

"What's with your brother?" she asked hesitantly. "Was that just an act?"

"Probably," I said, staring hard at the water. But the look in Jamie's grey eyes had somehow been unsettling. I tossed a pebble into the water. The ducks rose to half-mast, flapping their wings in alarm, but settled back to their sedate swim when nothing followed.

"Hi, Lori. Hi, Heather."

We both looked up. On the other side of the creek Cam Wright was walking his huge Great Dane.

"Hi!" we both yelled, waving.

"Is your chem done?" I added.

"Yeah." Cam grinned, then ran after his dog, which was suddenly chasing a passing bicycle.

Heather giggled. "Remember that awful crush I had on him in grade nine? Half the time I looked at him, he'd be looking at you."

"At *me*?"

"It used to make me so mad," she went on. "But you probably never even noticed because you were so crazy about Derek."

6

I picked another weed stalk. "Think Derek knew I was alive in grade nine?" I shut my eyes and Derek's face flashed before me — his daring blue eyes that could soften so unexpectedly, the clean square line of his jaw, the wispy blond moustache that was his pride and joy. The way he kissed was something else. I went quivery just thinking about it.

Heather's poke startled me. "Caught you daydreaming."

I grinned guiltily. But we'd been sitting too long. The chill of the wind probed my neck, and my hands felt just plain cold. I stood up. "Let's get moving."

Heather glanced at her watch. "Uh-oh! I didn't know it was so late. I still have to write that essay on *A Separate Peace.*" With a quick "See you later," she scrambled down the dike and was gone.

The roar of rush hour was in the air. Silvery church steeples gleamed in the afternoon sun. The mirror-panelled Bank of Montreal building downtown was a brilliant shaft defying the coming evening, and other tall buildings huddled together like gossiping kids. Farther out, hidden by the spread of city and trees, was the Saskatchewan prairie, stretching endlessly in all directions. Its vastness always seemed to mock the bustling city activity — and especially my own life. Here I was, sixteen years old, with everything I wanted, from a nice boyfriend to a loving family. But sometimes it seemed as if my life didn't stand for much. It was all too easy. By the time a person got to be sixteen, wasn't there supposed to be more to life than just having fun with friends and going to school?

I sighed and started home. My chemistry was done. So were my English and algebra assignments. Even the studying part was so easy that sometimes it got embarrassing.

\*   \*   \*

The warm, cheery smell of dinner greeted me when I got home. The table was set. But lying there with the plates and glasses was a trumpet with sections of tubing removed.

"Hi, Mom," I said as I kicked off my shoes. "Who messed up today?"

My mother gave me a tired smile. "Somebody had the bright idea of putting spitwads in Denise Hallek's horn when she was helping me pass out some new music." She pulled out the middle valve and frowned at the holes in the piston. "Yuk! She's growing algae in there!" She swabbed it, grimacing at the grunge that came out. "Oh — Derek called."

I sat down and picked up the trumpet. Back in my junior high days it had been embarrassing being the band teacher's daughter. But at least Mom had a homeroom too, and was respected as a good teacher.

Mom oiled the valve. "Call Jamie for supper, will you? And your dad too."

"This is delicious, Sheila," Dad said later as he dug into his stuffed zucchini.

Jamie and I exchanged glances. It *was* good — but sometimes it was hard to get excited about squash stuffed with healthy things like nuts and sunflower seeds and cheese.

Jamie poked at his food. "I'm not hungry."

"Eat your supper, Jamie," Dad said firmly. "I haven't seen a single bite make its way to your mouth, and the way you're growing you need it more than the rest of us."

"Derek's coming over," I said.

"Can you two really get any work done together?" Mom sounded sceptical.

I shrugged. "I'm already done. He just needs some help with the chemistry assignment." I turned on Jamie. "And no surprises, wiseguy, or I'll wring your scrawny neck."

But for some reason he didn't rise to the bait.

"Jamie," Mom said, "I'm afraid you'll have to use the patched sheets tonight. We wouldn't run into this problem if you didn't change them so often — you're going through sheets faster than my laundry schedule allows."

Jamie went a mottled red. "I can't help it if I get so sweaty! What'm I supposed to do, sleep in the bathtub?"

"Not a bad idea," I said. "It's better than wetting your bed every night."

His face turned so purple it looked as if his blood vessels were bursting. "I'm *not* wetting my bed!" His voice went hoarse and he stood up, banging against the table.

"Jamie," Dad said in a warning tone.

Mom had the evil eye fixed on me.

"Sorry," I muttered. And I was. Nearly every morning I saw Jamie hiding behind his bundle of soggy sheets as he rushed to the laundry hamper.

Jamie shot me a murderous look as he sat down again.

"I brought up the topic of after-death experiences in my developmental psychology class today," Dad said in a conversational tone. "The students were really interested. I think I'll carry on with more in my next lecture if —"

"You should get John to lecture for you," Jamie interrupted. "He had one, you know."

There was a stunned silence at the table. I stared at Jamie. His solemn face told me that, for once, he didn't have any tricks up his sleeve.

"He did," Jamie insisted. "Remember the harvesting accident when he fell off his uncle's combine? He died in the ambulance and they brought him back. He told me about it."

Something inside me shivered. I'd seen a couple of TV shows in which people had been interviewed and had described their experiences — who hadn't? But it was one thing to hear a stranger talking about coming face to face with a being of light, of unconditional love — God, maybe — and completely different to think of plain old John Duncan experiencing something like that.

Dad was stroking his beard, obviously deep in thought. "Would he mind talking to the class? It would be a rare opportunity."

"He'd probably chicken out," Jamie admitted, poking at his salad.

At that moment the phone rang. Both Jamie and I rushed to answer it but I was quicker. "Hello?" And then I grimaced and handed it to my brother. "It's your accomplice."

Jamie was unsteady on his feet as he grabbed the phone. I glanced from one parent to the other but they hadn't noticed. An instant later Jamie sat back down with a crash. "Can't we have dessert? John's coming over and we're gonna watch a show about the brain."

"Oh, yeah?" I muttered. "Derek's coming over and he'll want to use the TV for video games after we've checked our lab books."

Jamie snickered. "The Incredible Hunk. Brain the size of a banana seed, so he gets you to do his home—"

"Shut up!"

"Nobody's watching TV until the dishes are done," Mom said firmly. "I have tests to mark, so I'm exempt."

I sighed. If we didn't get moving I'd be stuck elbow-deep in suds when Derek arrived. "Maybe I'll skip dessert," I said, getting up to clear the table.

Jamie sighed dramatically. "Well, here's to the group effort." With his plate still half-full of food, he headed toward the kitchen. But he wobbled sideways against the door frame and the plate smashed to the floor.

I tiptoed past the confusion and began rinsing

dishes. Mom came up beside me with a pumpkin pie. I took a deep breath. "Why can't Jamie walk right anymore?"

She set the pie down so abruptly that I almost splashed it by mistake. "I wish I knew," she said after a long pause. She took a deep breath too. "I hope to God Dr. Mahler can get to the bottom of it all."

I was horrified. "You're taking him to Derek's dad?"

"He's the best in town," Mom said. "Dr. Olsen can't find anything wrong and he finally made a referral. Honestly, the way some doctors act as if they were God!" Her voice went tight. "The appointment's not until next month. I don't see why you have to wait so long to see a specialist." Her knuckles were white as she picked up a handful of silverware.

"What causes Jamie's night sweats?" I asked.

"I really don't know, Lori." Her voice was tinged with pain. She banged the forks and spoons into a saucepan. "I'm going to try to get him in earlier. What are people supposed to do, plan their illnesses around somebody else's schedule?"

Jamie swayed into the kitchen. We fell silent as he dumped chunks of the plate into the garbage.

Mom quickly made her hands busy. "Cut the pie, Lori."

But something in me was sluggish. I stood there looking at her.

"Are you gonna do it or not?" Jamie asked impatiently. Before I could reply, he gouged a knife into the pie. I watched sceptically as he dug in with the pie server. The first piece plopped onto the countertop.

"Brother! Are you ever co-ordinated today!"

Jamie's glaring eyes hinted that he'd overheard our conversation.

Mom took the utensils from Jamie's hands. "Sit down."

"See?" I said to him.

Jamie rolled his eyes inward until only the whites showed.

"Go!" Mom made shooing motions with her hands. "Out! Both of you! You're just in my way."

I brushed past my brother and he wobbled.

Mom looked sharply at him.

"Take me off to the drunk tank," Jamie sang. But his grey eyes were miserable.

\*     \*     \*

Jamie was the one who was elbow-deep in dishwater when the doorbell rang. I rushed to answer it but it was only John.

"Just a sec," he said as I turned away. There was an odd pucker between his eyebrows. "Has Jamie started drinking or something?"

"*What?*" The idea stunned me. "You'd know about it before me," I said slowly. "It's not like him."

"I know." John's grey-green eyes narrowed

behind his thick glasses. "Hey, Einstein," he called, "how come you can't get those dishes to wash themselves?"

"I could," Jamie yelled back. "But we need some kind of ultrasonic chamber. Or a dog."

I lingered in the entry. Now that John had arrived, Jamie wouldn't care whether I finished drying the dishes or not. And then Derek was at the door, books under his arm and smelling of aftershave. "You're that crazy about chem?" he asked with a grin.

I took his jacket. "It sure beats washing dishes with the brat and the great John Duncan."

Derek fingered his wispy moustache and gave me a sad-dog smile. "Aw, I thought you were waiting for *me*."

"Not a chance." I shoved against him a little.

"Too bad — must have the wrong house." He turned to go.

"Yeah, wrong house." I opened the door for him. "Sorry about that." And then we both cracked up laughing.

Derek put one hand between my shoulder blades and steered me toward the living room. "Prisoner, march."

"Hup, two, three, four, throw that chemistry out the door."

"Only the books." Derek grabbed me around the middle and pulled me down onto the chesterfield. With a startled "Meow!" our old black and white tomcat, Sir Thomas Catt, darted out from beneath it and escaped upstairs.

14

I leaned back against Derek. Right away I felt more all-there, just the two of us, his shoulder supporting me. He gave me a little squeeze. "Are they all busy?" he whispered.

Uneasiness wriggled through me. "I thought you wanted to study." Our living room was not a place where I felt comfortable kissing boyfriends. I glanced at my watch. "The brat and company will be in to watch TV in a few minutes."

"Why can't your parents buy another TV for your rec room?" Derek grumbled. "Or, for God's sake, what's so awful about you and me studying down there without the evil eye spying on us?"

"That's just the way it is." I reached for the books but made the mistake of looking at him halfway there. His blue eyes were so inviting that I melted.

"That's more like it," he murmured, and kissed me.

It was as if a curtain had dropped, closing Derek and me into a tiny private room. We drifted timelessly, with only a faint stodgy voice in the back of my mind telling me that there were other people around.

A whoop split the air. I jumped, banging my nose on Derek's forehead. Something cool and moist and slippery had oozed across my cheek and down beneath my collar. I glimpsed two smirking faces and an arm brandishing the bottle of dishwashing detergent. And then Mom was there.

Her eyes were snapping with fire. "Derek, if

15

that's your idea of studying, you'd better do it somewhere else. This is our home and you should be more considerate."

"Sorry, Mrs. Carmichael," he mumbled.

Humiliation and anger surged through me and I had to look away. Defending myself could only mean betraying Derek, so I kept quiet.

"Mom, you should make them study at the kitchen table," Jamie called through the open door. "One at each end, with you in the middle to referee."

"Shut up, brat!" I rose to my feet, fists clenched. "Jamie Carmichael, I'm going to peel your face off and flush it down the toilet!"

"I'd like to see you try." He grinned and squirted the dishwashing liquid in a miniature pink fountain.

Derek had collected himself. "I'm sorry, Mrs. Carmichael. It won't happen again. But I do need Lori's help with my homework. Can I stay long enough for that?"

"Oh, all right." Mom's voice had a bite to it. "But you watch it, young man." She glared at me. "Lori, I'll talk to you later."

At that moment Dad appeared with a handful of papers and psychology journals. He sat down in the reclining chair. I cringed and opened my lab book. My parents had never seemed to like Derek much. Now things were bound to get worse. What had Derek been thinking anyway, kissing me in our living room with the whole family *and* John Duncan underfoot?

Derek wiped his hand across the back of his neck. "Cripes, what'd they dump on us anyway?"

"Detergent," I muttered. "Probably to clean up our act."

He swore under his breath. I reached over to open his lab book. Damn that Jamie! I'd have to slip him a dose of the stuff in his milk at breakfast.

Derek sighed and picked up his book. "School's so boring. Why do they try to fill our minds with this garbage? All we do is forget it."

Something inside me rebelled. Chemistry was fun for me. It seemed miraculous the way all those tiny atoms and molecules fit together to make the world — and people. "I bet your dad didn't forget his chem," I said.

He stirred restlessly. "He's a doctor."

"The brat's got an appointment to see him," I said, staring hard at the toes of my socks. "He walks weird, and nobody can figure out why."

Derek glanced furtively at my father, then whispered, "I bet he's just on something."

"I don't think so." Annoyance sparked inside me. And then, unbidden, the image of Jamie sprawled on the creek bank reappeared to haunt me.

# 2
# Emergency

It was two weeks later and in the middle of the night when we realized exactly how wrong things were.

I awakened suddenly from a dream in which I'd been in a noisy arena, dressed in my bathing suit and ski boots. I had been searching for my French assignment, somehow lost on the ice, when behind me there had come the scraping clash of skates. I whirled around and came face to face with a monstrous goalie dressed in black and wearing a terrifying mask.

I lay there, frightened and suddenly wide awake. Far away I heard a siren. The street lights cast shadows across my window, bare branches swaying in the wind. I heard the bus go by three blocks away and knew that if I sat up in bed I'd be able to see its lighted windows glowing like eyes in the dark.

Something moved at the foot of my bed. A warm body marched up my legs to settle, purring, on my stomach. Absently my hand fondled the rounded frostbitten ear tips of Sir Thomas Catt.

There was a strange scraping sound in the hall.

I stiffened and lifted the cat off me so I could sit up to hear better. Without changing the volume of his purr, Sir Thomas came right back.

I'd just begun wondering whether I'd imagined the noise when it came again, just outside my door. Sir Thomas's purr died abruptly and his ears twitched. Prickles ran up the back of my neck. My heart was pounding unevenly. The cat jumped down and padded out into the hall to investigate.

I heard Jamie cough. "Git!" he said suddenly in a choked voice. "Think I like inhaling cat hair?"

Silence.

"*Move, fur-brain!* Make yourself useful and wake somebody up for me."

What was going on out there? I pulled the covers up to my chin and didn't move.

The scraping sound came again, followed by a grunt.

Shivering, I got up and flicked on the light. It spilled into the hallway, where I saw Jamie lying on the floor with Sir Thomas right beside him.

"Jamie! What happened?"

"Dumb legs!" The terrified tone of his voice shot into me like a tiny spinning vortex, sucking away my breath.

"Come on, I'll help you." I grasped him around the ribs and strained, lifting. My brother felt feverish and was drenched with sweat. "Come on! Expect me to do all the work myself? Get up."

"I *can't!*" Jamie's voice rose with frustration. "My legs won't work!"

I sighed and looked down at him. His straight hair clung to his forehead and temples in wet clumps, and his grey eyes stared back at me, glazed with panic. I crouched down and tried again. "How'd you ever get to be so heavy?"

Mom appeared at the end of the hall. "Jamie! What happened?"

Suddenly Jamie looked ready to cry. "I've got to go to the bathroom so bad it hurts, only nothing comes out. And then I fell down, and now I can't even get up again."

"Jim!" Mom's sharp cry hurt my ears. She turned to me. "Lori, go wake up your father."

The next few minutes stretched into an unreal series of actions frozen into nightmarish slow motion. Pulling on clothes over pyjamas, huddling into jackets, Dad picking Jamie up and carrying him downstairs. Everybody seemed to have forgotten about me, so I tagged along, feeling like a ghost.

At first the car wouldn't start. It choked and sputtered in the cold night. Then we rushed through streets that were nearly empty, cheating on red lights and taking some fast corners. The fluorescent pallor of the *Emergency* sign cast a chill into me, making me feel even less like a three-dimensional person. Jamie was whisked away on a gurney with Mom at his side. After Dad registered, he too disappeared. The nurse said I had to wait.

The magazines were all out of date. I flipped through them, unable to make sense of the words, unable to shake off the numbness and the grit-eyed feeling of too little sleep. I stared at folded wheelchairs parked along one wall. "Dr. Stark to Emergency," an impersonal female voice said through the intercom. "Dr. Stark to Emergency." A white-coated man paused at the nursing station, then headed toward the curtained-off examining rooms.

The clock on the wall was an old one that clicked and jumped each minute. I watched it slowly jerk its way from 3:58 to 4:17. If only Derek were with me — or Heather. With her I could talk about absolutely anything. I tried to imagine Jamie on an examining table and wondered what was being done to him, but my imagination didn't want to work.

After the longest time Dad came out. His face was a peculiar greyish colour and he was white around the mouth. "Jamie's being admitted," he said. "I'll take you home."

"What's wrong with him?" I asked.

There was a haunted look in his eyes. "I don't know."

What were we going to do, walk out and leave Jamie and Mom in this place of disinfectant smells and bustling strangers?

"Would you like to see him?" Dad seemed to have read my mind.

I nodded, although the idea made my stomach twist with nervousness.

Jamie was heavily sedated. His eyes blinked open when Dad and I came in. He just looked at me without speaking. He seemed so vulnerable lying there on the examining table, so unlike his usual energetic self that suddenly I was chewing my lower lip to keep from crying.

There was a strangled sound beside me. I glanced over at Mom. She was all wet around the eyes and her white-knuckled hands were clutching a very shredded tissue.

Jamie's eyelids drooped. In less than a minute he was snoring.

Dad gave me a look that said it was time to go. Then he turned to Mom. "You'll call if you need me?"

She pressed her fingertips to her temples and nodded. "Call the substitute office in plenty of time. Tell them to cancel band practice."

Dad's arm went around her for a long silent moment. He kissed her, then gently steered me out. As I passed Jamie I brushed against a plastic bag partially filled with an amber liquid, dangling from between the side rails of the narrow examining table. I nearly gagged when I realized what it was.

Our feet clattered in the empty hallway. "What did the doctor say?" I asked as we went out the door.

Dad's voice was weary. "I'll tell you at home, Lori."

We fell into a heavy silence. The cold air smelled of dying plant matter. I shivered. The killing frost was at work. High above us a crescent moon shone coldly. The city wasn't awake yet, and the traffic lights changed colours for empty streets.

At home the first thing Dad did was pour himself a drink. He sloshed the whiskey in his glass, staring at it. I sat waiting. Sir Thomas Catt materialized from under the chesterfield and settled in my lap.

Dad stared and swallowed, stared and swallowed. I felt like poking him to see if that would make him speak. Across the street a light flicked on. John Duncan's father was a milkman and always got up early.

Dad drank the final swallow. "Lori," he said hoarsely, "your brother is paralyzed."

Shock reeled through me in a clammy wave. Everything was limp — my arms, my legs, my mind.

"The doctor thinks something must be pressing against his spinal cord." Dad was speaking again, but his words sounded like a TV in a distant room. "They'll do a myelogram to see where the problem is and then probably operate."

My mouth opened but questions refused to form. My hands were sweaty on Sir Thomas's back. He pulled away and began licking himself.

Dad's sigh was like air hissing out of a balloon. "Dr. Stark has no idea what's causing it. I guess we won't know any more until after the surgery."

I just sat there.

"Go back to bed, Lori," he said in a gentle tone. The rest of his words blurred as I stood up obediently.

Numbly I went upstairs. Once in bed I felt I ought to cry or something. But I couldn't. Something in me was alien. What was happening couldn't be real. I tried thinking of Derek to relax. It didn't work. I reviewed the molecular structures from our past chemistry experiments. Covalent bonding. Ionic bonding. I turned the light on and tried to read. That didn't work either. My mind kept spinning like car wheels on ice.

Finally I got up and wrote it all down for Heather. I could hand her the note when we met at our lockers before I had English and she had typing, and then we could talk it over on our way to gym.

* * *

I might as well have skipped school that day. I felt unable to connect with anything going on around me. Teachers' voices droned in a garbled blur. I sat there like a clump of leftover oatmeal. Finally everyone decided I was in a bad mood and left me alone. I couldn't even bring myself to give Heather the three-page note, knowing I'd have to talk about it later. So I slipped it through the vents in her locker just after the final bell, then ran madly to the bus stop so I'd miss Derek too.

There was standing room only on the bus. My body swayed and lurched with the ride and I tried to stay loose so I wouldn't go staggering off balance. I rode on past our street. After calling home about ten times during the day and getting no answer there or at Dad's office at the university, it seemed simplest to go straight to the hospital. The idea of facing an empty house when everything was so terribly wrong seemed even deadlier than telling my friends what was on my mind.

It was awful walking into the hospital all by myself, awful asking at the information desk for Jamie's room number. But worst of all was walking down corridors of sick people, looking for room 437. It gave me a feeling of trespassing, going past rooms with signs like *Oxygen: no smoking*. Through open doors I could see beds with strangers who didn't seem real. There was a drabness about the whole place that never showed up in hospital stories on TV. It left me afraid to look at the patients — and why should I? They weren't part of my life.

Then I was standing in the doorway of room 437. In one bed lay an old man who was snoring loudly. There was Mom sitting in a chair, her head drooping. The patient in the other bed was lying on his stomach, turned away from me. The hospital gown parted slightly, revealing a bandage in the middle of his back. Was that Jamie? In a frightening way the hospital gown made him seem like just one more of the countless strangers I'd hurried past on my way in. I tiptoed into the room.

A bottle of intravenous fluid was suspended from a pole at Jamie's bedside, dripping slowly into clear plastic tubing that dangled across the sheets until it vanished beneath another bandage on his arm. I winced.

"Owww," he moaned softly.

My skin prickled and seemed to shrink. I crept around to the other side of his bed so he could see me. "Hi," I mumbled, at a loss for anything more original to say.

Jamie's eyes were bright with pain. "Go find a nurse," he said in a whiny voice. "Tell her I hurt. And I'm thirsty."

Mom's head jerked up. She blinked at me. "Lori — I'm glad you came." Her face was haggard. She looked as if she had aged ten years overnight.

"I hurt," Jamie said again.

Mom looked at her watch. "I don't think they can give you anything, hon," she said in a helpless voice. "It's only been two hours."

Jamie moaned and swore.

I took a couple of steps backwards. In the other bed Jamie's roommate stirred, then resumed his steady snore. I turned to Mom. "What did they find out?" I asked hesitantly.

She sighed heavily.

"I've got the intergalactic invasion of the extra-terrestrials," Jamie said in a thick voice.

"What?" Was he so doped up that he didn't know what he was talking about or was he just trying to be funny?

26

"There was a lymph node pressing against his spinal cord." Mom sounded tired and confused. "An inter— interco—"

"Intercostal node causing extradural compression," Jamie finished up for her.

I sagged against the wall. "So what's that supposed to mean?"

Jamie closed his eyes and didn't move. With a warning look, Mom slowly shook her head.

A million questions bombarded me, questions I couldn't ask right then. I looked helplessly at Mom. And all she did was silently shake her head.

"Will you cut the crap?" Jamie said irritably, his eyes still shut. "If you want to talk about me, talk. Or go. I don't need a babysitter and I'm not gonna do something dumb like falling out of bed."

Mom flinched.

"Mom?" I said uncertainly. "Want a cup of coffee?"

She managed a weary smile. "No thanks, Lori. I've had so much coffee already that I'm wired."

"Where's Dad?" I asked.

She glanced at her watch. "At the university. He had a graduate seminar he couldn't cancel. He just left. He was here when the doctor came around to see us and he was able to spend a couple of hours with Jamie after the operation."

Chalk up one more person I couldn't run to. "I think I'll go home," I said, needing to escape.

"You'll be all right?" Mom sounded concerned but too tired to get up.

"Yeah." Since there was obviously nothing I could do to help Jamie feel better, and since I couldn't find out the most important things, I'd be better off taking a long run — or catching a bus to the university where I could hit tennis balls against a backboard.

"You go too, Mom," Jamie muttered. "I'm tired of being looked at and poked. I'm not some new species of bacteria under a microscope, you know."

Mom sat there looking as if she were trying not to cry.

"I'm okay," Jamie said irritably. "If you'd go, maybe I could sleep."

"I could do with some of that myself," my mother said wearily. "All right, Jamie, you win. We'll be in to see you after supper."

"What's wrong with him?" I asked once we were safely down the hall.

Her voice was brittle. "He has a condition called Hodgkin's disease. Don't worry, it's not contagious. It's a disease that makes the lymph nodes swell up. They took the node off his spine but he hasn't recovered sensation in his legs yet. The doctor says it's possible he may regain complete function but it's too early to know one way or the other."

So he was paralyzed, at least for now. For the second time the news shook me. I felt like a robot, staring at the lighted buttons in the elevator, moving down corridors that might as well have been blank walls. But I was jolted out of my daze when Mom stumbled going down the outside steps. I grabbed her elbow. "Mom! Are you all right?"

"Would you drive home, Lori?" she asked. "I'm so tired I can hardly even see." When we arrived home she went straight upstairs.

I looked at the solar energy kit that Jamie and John had left on the coffee table. Did John know what was going on? Chances were he didn't. Suddenly the walls seemed to be closing in around me. I grabbed my tennis racquet and a can of balls, only to meet Derek coming up the front steps.

"Hey! What's going on? Why the brush-off today?"

Bewildered, I looked at him. Probably Derek didn't know what was going on either. Not yet anyway. "Come hit some balls with me," I said after a blank pause.

He shot me a pained look. "Are you crazy? You hardly talk to me all day and now you want to go run around on a tennis court? It's below freezing."

On top of everything else, was I going to be stuck arguing with Derek? "I have to," I said in a jittery voice. "You'll understand."

"Okay." He sounded sceptical. "Get your dad's racquet."

The courts were empty and clear except for a few icy patches. The cool air slashed away some of the fuzz clouding my brain as I half crouched in ready position. Derek was a good player and

29

sometimes could leave me standing there in disbelief when he used his wicked spin.

"What's going on anyway?" he called after we were warmed up.

I served into the net and kicked at the baseline. "It's Jamie." And then I let him have it, a serve that sliced over the net and skidded across his backhand corner.

"Hey!" he yelped. "Go a little easy! I didn't come here to get creamed."

"Serves you right, asking questions before we're done playing." And I followed with a gentle serve that barely made it over the net. "Hah — thirty-love."

He glowered at me and I knew he'd send me some real sizzlers in the next game. We got into a long rally. I rushed to the net as soon as I could. Then Derek lobbed. I watched the ball coming like a tiny green moon and ran backwards, trying to calculate the best spot for a return. If I smashed —

My shoe slipped on ice and the ball hit the handle of my racquet. I was falling, twisting. Then came the grinding crunch of concrete against my skull.

The fiery pain brought tears to my eyes and a ringing in my ears. Gingerly I touched the spot, expecting to see blood on my fingertips. But there was none. On my scalp I felt the beginnings of a huge lump.

"Lori!" Derek grasped my shoulders.

"I'm okay." Dazed, I struggled to get up.

"Not so fast, eh?" His eyes were worried. Carefully he touched the tender spot. "That's gonna be a mean one. Better get some ice on it."

I gestured at the court. "There's plenty right here — shall I kneel down and apply my bump to it?" But when I tried to laugh, tears came instead.

"Lori, you're hurt."

"No, I'm not. It's just Jamie. He's —" It was too much. My head came down on his shoulder and I cried.

"Lori?" Derek sounded nervous, maybe because I'd never cried on him before. But with the bump on my head and Jamie — *paralyzed?* — with some disease I'd never heard of before, the whole world was turned upside down.

"Lori, I'd better take you to my dad."

I pulled away and hiccupped. "No! I'm okay!"

"Then what's wrong? You said something about your brother?"

I blinked through the tears and nodded, trying to pull myself together.

Derek patted my head awkwardly. I winced, hoping he wouldn't hit the bruise. "What's wrong with Jamie?" he went on.

"He's paralyzed," I choked out. "Your dad operated on him this morning and nobody knows if he'll get his legs back or not."

There was a long silence in which a jet went overhead and plenty of traffic sped by on the Trans-Canada Highway. "God," he said at last. He seemed to have nothing more to say.

Suddenly I was nervous. "Take me home. Mom's all in a frazzle and she probably needs company."

Without a word he collected our gear and took me home.

Then Heather called and I had to explain it to her as well. But the hardest part was when John Duncan wandered in looking for Jamie. When I told him the news he sagged back against the door as if he'd been shot. His eyes filled with tears. And there wasn't a thing I could do to help him.

# 3
# Cancer!

As the week wore on I got used to answering questions about Jamie and life settled down a bit. Heather hovered around me like a mother hen, while Derek tried to act as if nothing was wrong. I needed both perspectives. But when Derek surprised me with what I hadn't known about Jamie, everything fell apart all over again.

The hallway was noisy with slamming locker doors. I must have been walking fast because Derek suddenly grasped my arm. "Slow down, okay? This isn't a race track."

I laughed a little and grinned up at him. "Sorry. Everything's been so crazy, sometimes I don't know if I'm coming or going."

He looked away. "I guess that's understandable, finding out someone in your family has cancer."

I stopped dead. "Oh, no," I said. Thank goodness Derek was beginning to talk about it with me — but how could he have gotten it so wrong? "Jamie's got Hodgkin's disease."

He stuffed his hands into his back pockets and gave me the oddest look. "Hodgkin's disease *is* cancer," he said.

My hands went sweaty around my notebooks. "No, it's not," I said, watching Wendy go out the front door.

Derek's face was troubled. "Didn't anybody tell you?"

"Tell me what?" My head was buzzing inside and I wished he would get on with whatever he was trying to say. My notebooks slipped and scattered on the floor. Both of us bent to pick them up. The look on Derek's face burned into my mind, too pink, and guilty.

"Hodgkin's disease is cancer," he repeated. "Cripes, I thought everybody knew that."

Suddenly the noisy hallway seemed to be shouting at me, while the people in it might as well have been made of cardboard. I felt a bit like cardboard myself, unable to process the information Derek had just given me.

"I thought you already knew," Derek said weakly. "I never would've said anything if —"

I turned quickly, dodging people as I rushed away. Derek was calling me but I kept going, needing to be alone. Outside, the bus was waiting at the curb. I made a run for it, but when I was halfway there it pulled away. I kept running and nearly collided with a slow-moving pickup turning into a side street.

I ran until my side ached. Then I slowed, exhausted. Without realizing it, I had been heading in the direction of the hospital. I sank down on a bus stop bench to rest and wondered whether I should go see Jamie. Did he know he had cancer? A deep shudder went through me, and it had nothing to do with the chill November air.

The sky was shrouded with soft grey. Probably it would snow soon. My cross-country skis were waiting in the basement. But Jamie — *cancer?* No. It couldn't be. Maybe Derek didn't know what he was talking about. Mom and Dad would've told me. *Would* they have told me? My kid brother in hospital, paralyzed — with *cancer?* I began to shiver and couldn't stop. Was Jamie going to die?

A pickup pulled into the bus zone. I ignored it.

"Hey, Lori!"

It was Cam. I refused to look at him, wishing he'd go away. But his door slammed.

"What's up?" he asked. How much did Cam know? I wondered. Had he known all along too? I stared at a smashed cigarette butt on the sidewalk. Cam sat down on the bench beside me. "Hey, lady, you just about put some expensive dents in my truck."

"What?" I still couldn't stop shivering.

His brown eyes didn't reveal a thing about what he did or didn't know. "You just about broadsided me after you missed the bus. Ever think of getting insurance?"

"Who needs insurance?" I muttered.

He picked up my books. "I'll give you a lift to the hospital. I'm headed that way anyhow."

"Who says that's where I'm going?" My voice came out with a rude abruptness but I didn't care.

"Why else would you be waiting for a bus in this part of town?"

His matter-of-fact tone convinced me. I shrugged and got into his pickup. At least it would be warmer than sitting there in the cold.

He swerved out into the traffic and found a spot in the faster lane. I sat there, jolting with every bump in the street.

"Sorry about that," Cam said. "Shocks're going." He lit up a cigarette.

"I'm not going to your funeral," I muttered.

He didn't reply. In the close quarters of the truck cab the cigarette smoke was soon prickling my throat. I started coughing and cranked down the window. It was starting to snow.

The brakes screeched as Cam parked in a stall marked *Ambulances Only*. "Here you are."

"Thanks," I said stiffly, reaching for my books.

Snowflakes tickled my eyelashes when I got out. Cam got out too.

"What're you doing?" I asked.

He glanced at me. "You're not in such a wonderful mood, are you?"

"Well, what do you expect? I didn't know — I just found out that Hodgkin's disease is really —" My voice caught in my throat.

"Yeah, I know. It must be pretty tough on you." He sounded embarrassed. "Hey, do you know where X-ray is? I'm supposed to pick up my granddad."

36

Suddenly tears were threatening to spill. I turned away without answering.

Jamie was laughing when I walked into his green-walled room. John Duncan was sitting in the visitor's chair laughing too. His empty backpack lay on the floor.

*Did Jamie know?* The question sliced through me once again. I turned away sharply and leaned against the radiator.

"Hello, stranger," John said.

"He tickles!" Jamie's voice was hoarse with laughter.

"Don't let him get away!"

My throat tightened. Probably neither of them knew the bad news. Jamie seemed to be coping amazingly well with the paralysis. Mom and Dad had been emphasizing the possibility that it might be temporary, that damaged nerve tissue sometimes required a few days to recover. But even so, it was hard to look at Jamie's motionless legs.

Jamie scowled at me. "What's the matter with you, buffalo face?"

I couldn't tell him. "See you," I muttered and went out the door.

John followed. "What's wrong?" Unlike Derek and most of the kids at school, John seemed able to look me straight in the eye without getting embarrassed.

I stalled. A staircase was nearby — maybe I could make a quick run for it. But John kept right on looking at me. I drew in a deep breath. "Do you know?"

Suddenly John's eyes were guarded. He pushed his hair back from his forehead and his foot started tapping in a fidgety manner. "Know what?"

I took another breath. "That Hodgkin's disease is cancer." My mouth was dry and I was trembling.

"Didn't you know?" John sounded stunned. "Jamie told me the very first day I came in."

I sagged and shook my head, and looked hard at the wall because my eyes were brimming.

"Hey," John said awkwardly, touching my shoulder, "it's curable."

"J.D.!" Jamie yelled. "C'mere! Quick!"

John dashed back into Jamie's room. I stood there feeling numb. But a young nurse swished past on nearly silent feet and gave me a nice smile. "Jamie's doing very well," she said. "Doctor says he'll be home in a few days."

Home for what? Life in a wheelchair? With cancer? I drew in another deep breath and took a few steps toward the stairway.

"You still there, Lor?" Jamie called in a grouchy voice.

"Yeah." I went back in reluctantly and looked more closely at my brother. The IV was gone. Jamie sat propped up against several pillows. Something at the foot of his bed held the covers up and away from his feet.

"Holy —" he said, shaking his head. "You didn't know?"

I sat down on the radiator. "Derek told me."

"The Incredible Hunk actually knows something besides video games." A malicious glint flashed in my brother's eyes.

"You be quiet." I picked at a strip of loose paper sticking out through the metal spiral of my notebook. "John says it's curable?" I asked after a long silence.

"Sometimes." For a moment Jamie's face was vulnerable and his voice was scared. He shifted in bed. "They still need to do a bunch of tests. I've got something on one lung. Tomorrow they'll cut me between the toes and shoot in dye to see if I've got it anywhere else. Then they'll give me chemotherapy called MOPP and I'll go bald."

A heavy silence permeated the air.

"Still working on wiggling your toes, J.C.?" John asked at last.

Jamie didn't reply. His expression shut me out completely. With a jolt I realized some of the horrors he must be facing entirely on his own in that hospital bed. I looked at his legs, lying still beneath the sheets. Something else was under the covers. As I watched, that lump twitched and then wiggled toward the outline of Jamie's legs. I stared. "What's that?"

"Medical secret," John said solemnly.

But something told me otherwise. "Uh-huh. Knowing you two, it's probably a boa constrictor."

*"Felis domesticus,"* Jamie said in a half-hearted voice.

"Meow." The lump spoke for itself and writhed furiously. I gasped. John doubled over

39

laughing. Jamie's face relaxed and a trace of his normal devilish glint lurked in his eyes. Sir Thomas Catt poked his head out from under the covers, his black ears flattened back in anger. He glared at me and, before anybody could stop him, darted under the bed.

"Oops." Jamie smothered a giggle and bit his lower lip. John dived under the bed just as a huffy starched nurse strode into the room.

She gave Jamie and me the evil eye. "It's awfully noisy in here," she said coldly, frowning at John's outstretched legs.

Sir Thomas let out an ominous cat growl.

Jamie went into a spasm of fake coughing. The nurse stood there like a prison guard. "I would like you to come out from under the bed, young man."

"Jamie dropped something." John's muffled voice had a telltale guilty ring. "Oh — there it is."

But the nurse didn't go.

Jamie's grey eyes darted from one thing in the room to another. "It's too hot in here," he said. "Can't you open the windows for some fresh air?" I looked out at the falling snow and tried to keep a straight face.

"When is my lymphangiogram?" Jamie continued. "Is it true the dye turns your urine and your face green?"

"Yes," the nurse replied curtly, still glaring at John's legs.

John seemed to be groping for something. I

looked around, wondering what it might be. The backpack! With a gentle kick I sent it under the bed. A moment later John slid out, his glasses crooked and his hair mussed.

The nurse gave him a scathing look. "I've warned you, young man. This is not a schoolyard. Any more nonsense and you will have to leave."

John's face went crimson. "Sorry." The backpack was squirming. Quickly he tucked it under his arm and leaned against the wall.

"Don't let it happen again." Like an insulted queen, the nurse left the room.

Jamie stuck his tongue out at her back.

"Ow!" John hissed. "Watch those claws, cat!" He shoved the pack under the covers.

Jamie's eyes widened suddenly. "Hey! Cut it out, you —" He broke off. A wildly hopeful look was burning in his face. "He's biting me," he said in a tiny voice.

"So?" But then John whisked the covers away. All three of us looked at the cat curled around my brother's foot, hanging on with claws and teeth.

"You felt that?" I whispered.

John let out a whoop and too late clapped a hand over his mouth. "All right!" He pounded the bed. "Can you wiggle your toes?"

I lifted the old black and white cat off my brother's feet. "Can you?"

A look of intense concentration settled in Jamie's face. Holding my breath, I watched his feet. Red streaks appeared where Sir Thomas had scratched him. And then, very slowly, the big toe on Jamie's right foot wiggled back and forth.

"You did it!" I gasped. Sir Thomas was squirming to get free.

"The other one too?" John looked so happy I was afraid he'd lift my brother right out of bed. "All right, J.C.!"

Swift footsteps silenced us. Just in time I stuffed the poor cat back into the bag. "I warned you," the nurse began.

"Nurse," Jamie said politely, "I can move my toes."

"I'd better get outta here." John gave my brother a playful thump on the head and made a hasty exit.

"Wait!" I cried. In the backpack Sir Thomas's weight shifted precariously. Tucking it against me, I followed John.

"I can't believe it," he said over and over again as we took the elevator to the first floor.

After the initial surprise, relief had spilled through me in a giddy rush. Maybe Jamie would walk again. Maybe the cancer would go away and everything would get back to normal. Derek and I would be able to relax together, instead of trying to pretend nothing had changed. Maybe we could all go right back to where we'd been before. "Mom and Dad will be so happy," I murmured. But suddenly I choked up. "I just don't understand why they never told me it was cancer."

The dancing excitement drained from John's eyes. He gave me a sympathetic smile.

"It's actually curable?" There was a little catch in my voice. "I always thought if you got cancer . . ."

"His kind's pretty good — something like eighty percent curable if you catch it early."

I went a little weepy. John noticed and put his hand on my shoulder. But I didn't mind. If only Derek had done it when I'd needed it. After all, Jamie's illness was turning out to be quite a crisis — and I'd always thought Derek would be more sensitive.

John and I walked silently to the bus stop. Snowflakes sifted through bare treetops, carpeting sidewalks and lawns. Tires hissed and left black stripes on white. Snow flecked John's dark hair and speckled my notebooks. We didn't talk until the bus came.

Arguing voices floated downstairs to greet me as I walked in the front door — Mom and Dad. I tensed.

"Is she home?" Mom asked suddenly in a guarded tone.

I froze in the immediate quiet, suddenly filled with resentment. Why hadn't they told me about the cancer? Let them argue — I could share the good news later.

As Dad's voice resumed, I sank to a crouching position near the foot of the stairs. ". . . really should tell her," he was saying. "After all, the treatment is extensive. Besides, she deserves to know."

Mom said something in a low voice.

"She's hardly a child anymore," Dad continued. "She's bound to find out sooner or later anyway, and how will she feel if she finds out from somebody else?"

I took a deep breath. "I found out today," I said loudly. My voice had a sullen sound.

Two shocked and apologetic faces appeared at the top of the stairs. "Lori, I'm sorry." Mom's voice broke. "I only wanted to protect you. I thought —"

"Yeah, I know," I said heavily. Suddenly I was tired and it was impossible to stay angry. "Jamie can feel in his feet again and wiggle his toes."

Mom burst into tears. Dad's exclamation went right past me. The whole day was turning out to be so emotionally draining that I just couldn't handle any more. I tightened the laces on my running shoes and went out the back door to run in the falling snow.

# 4

# Chain reactions

The idea for the ski weekend came up when everybody was over at our house. We were in the rec room downstairs and it was like having our own private world — although every time someone got up to change a cassette I could hear Mom playing the piano. Jamie had begun his chemotherapy on an outpatient basis and had spent half the afternoon throwing up. At first Mom had followed him around, trying to be helpful, but he got so fed up he just about bit her head off. The minute supper was over, Mom had retired to the piano to play some crashy Chopin.

"Everybody planning to be home over Christmas?" Wendy asked during a lull in the conversation.

Derek quit trying to tickle my feet. "Not if my old lady gets her way. She's pestering the old man to go to Barbados."

Wendy's pert face grew reflective. "I was thinking. My uncle's got a place in Blefeld —"

"Blefeld?" Debi hooted. "That place is abandoned!"

"Not my uncle's farm," Wendy retorted. "Anyway, he's spending the winter in Phoenix and I was thinking — wouldn't it be fun if we all went out there and skied for a couple of days?"

"All right!" Alan stood up and stretched. "Blefeld, here we come!" A wicked grin flashed across his face. "No chaperones?"

Wendy had just filled her mouth with chips. "Oh, come on!" she sputtered, swatting at him with the empty chip bag. "My parents would go too."

I stayed stretched out on my stomach. A ski trip would be the perfect escape. Things had been pretty crazy ever since the news of Jamie's illness, and if today had been any indication of what was to come, they were bound to get worse. "Sounds good to me." But I shot a longing look at Derek. It wouldn't be half as much fun without him.

"Well?" Wendy gestured toward the others. "What about the rest of you? Speak up!"

"I'll have to ask," Heather said cautiously. "You know my parents." There was a wistful note in her voice.

Cam had been unusually quiet all evening. "Count me in, I guess," he said. He seemed to have other things on his mind. Heather and I both glanced at him, but Derek slipped an ice cube down the back of my shirt. The streak of cold got me writhing on the floor, and then of course Derek had to do the honours of removing it for me.

46

" . . . new car for Christmas," Debi was saying when I'd recuperated. "I'll drive it there and show you guys."

Suddenly Derek was all ears. "What kind?" he asked. I might as well have dissolved into the carpet. A perverse urge to punch him flicked through me.

"Probably a Mustang." Debi's voice was off-hand. "I really want a TransAm, but you know how parents are."

"How about over New Year's?" Wendy persisted.

Cam was lighting a cigarette. "May as well."

I sighed. "Cam, my parents don't allow smoking, remember?"

"Sorry, I forgot." He looked around for an ashtray but naturally there weren't any.

Debi was eyeing me with a scornful look that implied my parents were full of it. I felt like telling her to cram it, but then everybody would wonder what had gotten into me.

"Another pair of lungs saved from cancer," Wendy said cheerfully. And then she remembered Jamie. "I'm sorry." She looked away, embarrassed.

Cam stood there in the sudden hush, staring at his cigarette.

"Here." I reached for it and poked it through the neck of my Pepsi bottle. "Junk into junk food," I said and grinned at Cam. "You weren't that hard up for a smoke, were you?"

Without answering, he turned and went over to look at the collection of tapes.

Derek was reaching for the bottle. "Pepsi, anyone?"

Heather covered her mouth and giggled. "Gross!"

Wendy caught the giggles too. "You guys! Want us throwing up all over the place?"

"I'll try it on my brother," I said, trying to keep my voice light. "He's been throwing up all day anyway."

There was a dead silence. Hot colour crept into my face. I got up and flushed the mess down the toilet.

"How come the medicine makes him so sick?" Wendy asked when I got back.

I sat down, wishing Derek would put his arm around me. But he didn't. I shivered and tucked my knees to my chest. It was still hard to talk about. "It kills cells," I said, wiggling my toes in the carpet. "Dad says the cells lining the stomach are really sensitive."

Over by the stereo Cam was listening intently, but he didn't speak.

"At least it's curable," Heather said. She gave me a reassuring smile. I needed it.

A spasm crossed Cam's face, as if he were in pain. He quickly balled one hand into a fist and started picking at a scab on his knuckle.

Everybody noticed. The room was absolutely still when the tape ended. Upstairs Mom had switched from Chopin to Scott Joplin, which she was banging out so carelessly that it almost sounded sarcastic.

Wendy broke the silence. "What's wrong, Cam?"

"He just needs that smoke," Debi scoffed.

But Cam was shaking his head. He picked off a bit of scab and flicked it across the room. "My granddad's got it," he muttered.

"Got what?" Alan asked.

Cam just stared at us with a strangely hostile expression.

Suddenly I knew. A trembling began deep inside me the way it always did whenever I really thought about Jamie. "Has he got cancer too?" I scooted closer to Derek, wishing he'd touch me — anything to push back the awful coldness.

But he didn't. "Cripes!" he burst out. "Why didn't you say something?" He almost sounded mad at Cam.

Something like anger snapped in Cam's dark eyes. "I just did, Mahler."

Debi made a face. "This evening's turning into a real bummer."

I tensed. "Well, if that's the way you feel —" But I bit back the rest. Everybody more or less tolerated Debi. Her mother was now with her fourth husband, and some of Debi's stepfathers had been real losers.

"Reality therapy," Derek said blandly.

Cam headed for the stairs. "I'm leaving."

He was probably hurting just the way I did over Jamie. I followed him. "Cam, are you okay?"

"Of course I'm okay!" he said sharply. But he was acting so unlike himself that I had a feeling it was bad news.

"Did you just find out?" I asked hesitantly, remembering the X-rays he'd mentioned the time he dropped me off at the hospital.

Cam sighed. "His lungs are a mess." For an instant he looked so vulnerable. "That old man's the only dad I ever had."

My eyes blurred and I felt like hugging him.

"I'd better go." He bundled up in his down jacket.

I followed him out the door. The night was still and crisp. I shivered at the first shock of coldness, then made my abdominal muscles relax so I wouldn't turn into a hunched over mass of goosebumps and chattering teeth.

Cam looked down at me. "For Chrissakes, Lori, you'll freeze your backside off! It must be minus twenty."

I took in a slow breath of frigid air. "I just wanted to say — if you ever need to talk, I know what it feels like." And then I was shivering, but whether from the cold or from the cancer talk I couldn't tell.

"Yeah. Maybe I will someday." He turned abruptly and headed for his pickup, looking so incredibly lonely that I was tempted to run after him.

I couldn't bring myself to go straight back downstairs to my friends. In the living room Jamie was walking with grim, determined steps toward the encyclopedia set. A plastic washbasin sat on the chesterfield. Sir Thomas Catt materialized from somewhere and rubbed, purring, against my ankles. But Jamie ignored me, so I didn't wait around.

"What should we do for him?" Heather asked in a subdued voice.

I gestured helplessly. "The same as for me, I guess." But I didn't look at Derek. If he treated Cam's situation the way he'd been treating mine, Cam would find himself awfully lonely.

"He'll handle it," Derek said easily. "Look at Lori — she's a real trooper."

My face tightened. Derek's casual manner was beginning to make me wonder exactly how much time he spent thinking about his friends. I glanced at Heather. Comprehension suddenly sparked in her eyes but it wasn't a time we could talk.

"This year's getting heavy," Alan muttered.

Wendy sighed. "Is it ever. But let's plan on Blefeld. It'll give us something fun to think about."

Everybody straggled upstairs. As usual, Derek was last to leave. Standing there beside the coat closet, he kissed me. But something in me held back.

"What's the matter?" he demanded.

"Just thinking about Cam." I couldn't tell Derek of the pain I'd sensed.

"Cam? What for?"

"You know. Because."

"What'd he say?" he asked suspiciously.

I sighed. "Nothing you haven't heard." But had Derek actually heard?

"Okay, so what'd you say?"

Resentment shot through me. "That if he ever needs to talk, I know what it feels like."

"Oh, for God's sake, Lori, why'd you go and say something dumb like that?"

I twisted away. "Because you need to be able to talk about that kind of thing."

"So what's the problem? Don't I let you talk enough? Then talk!"

"Heather lets me talk," I said stiffly. "And if Cam needs to talk, I can listen."

Derek made an impatient sound.

"You don't need to be jealous." Tears started sliding down my cheeks.

"Then prove it." Derek moved so he could see my face. "Oh, cripes, you're crying."

I broke down further, needing so badly for him to hold me.

"Look, Lori, I'm sorry." He patted my shoulder awkwardly. "Look, I don't know what to do when — oh, for God's sake, will you cut it out?"

I held out my arms to him, but instead of holding me, he went back to kissing me.

After a few minutes I felt better. But then came the unmistakable sound of vomiting in the living room.

Derek pulled back. "Oh, for God's sake! You'd think this place was a hospital!"

"Jamie's sick, remember?" I said coldly. Unable to take any more, I stepped into the living room just as my kid brother sagged back on the chesterfield. The front door slammed.

"So the Incredible Hunk couldn't take it, eh?" Jamie's voice was drained.

For an instant I hated him. It almost seemed as if he'd done it on purpose. But it wasn't Jamie's fault he was sick. I closed my eyes and leaned against the wall. "No," I said. "He couldn't take it."

# 5

# Mixed emotions

I awakened one Saturday morning to a sky that was still pink and white. I just lay there for a few minutes, cozy and warm. The poplar branches outside my window were coated with new snow. The house was quiet until the furnace went on with a rattle, followed by a whoosh of warm air through the vents.

I got up, dressing quietly and avoiding the creaky spots as I crept downstairs to pull on my outside gear. With skis and poles tucked under one arm, I went out the front door. Clean cold air greeted me. The snow lay smooth and unbroken by tire tracks or boot prints. I slipped into my skis.

Except for the ever-present sparrows and somebody's cat, I was in my own private world. I skied to the end of the block, where I worked my way sideways up the creek dike, leaving behind a jumble of skinny rib-like tracks. The sun was just casting its first gold rays across the faded weed stalks poking through the snow, while other

54

areas remained in chalk-blue shadow. The creek was frozen over, its surface softened by the new-fallen snow, except for a few icy grey-green patches bared by the wind.

Someone had already skied along the dike. I drew in an energizing breath and slipped into the fluid gliding motion, my skis hissing comfortably along the trail. Warmth came to my knees, to my upper arms, while the brisk air streamed past my face, blowing back the loose ends of my hair. I skimmed along faster still, suddenly free of the strain of the past month or so.

I skied past the giant willow and the wooden footbridge, past the concrete drainpipe. I skied until the utter freedom of movement gave way to the feeling of being overheated. My breath pumped out in white clouds. I glided to a halt.

I looked down the short steep slope of the dike, crouched, pushed off again and cannon-balled down. I flew, letting my knees absorb the bounces. I lost track of how many times I took the slope, and was beginning to tire when I pushed off for the last time. In the distance a huge dog was bounding ahead of its master. Was it Cam? Distracted, I forgot to shift my weight to allow for the deeper snow at the bottom of the slope — and landed face down, spread-eagled in the snow. The cold wetness shocked my cheeks. Fortunately nothing hurt. I rolled over and was greeted by a gigantic dog muzzle.

"Hey!" I sputtered. But the dog cut me off with a slurp on the mouth.

"Duke! Back!"

There was Cam, leash dangling loosely from one hand. "Lori! Are you all right?"

"Yeah." Sheepishly I got up.

He grinned and turned his gaze to the dog. "Duke. Sit." The huge animal obeyed.

"Are you sure he's not part horse?" I asked.

Cam laughed. "My nephew rides him."

I took a calming breath. "Does he bite?"

"My dog or my nephew?" He laughed again and swung the leash gently. "My nephew does. My dog doesn't."

An awkward silence fell.

"You're up early," I said.

"Duke needs his walk. What's your excuse?"

"I just woke up, that's all." For some reason I felt oddly shy.

Cam snapped his fingers at his dog and began walking. His voice seemed nervous. "How's your brother?"

Tightness clamped around my throat as I skied alongside him. "Okay, I guess. He hates his chemotherapy. His hair's starting to fall out. But he's bratty as ever." I hesitated. "How about your grandfather?"

Cam wouldn't look at me and his tone was guarded. "He's over his operation. Would you believe they took a whole lung? And now he's getting radiation." He paused, then went on in a low voice. "What makes me so mad is nobody'll say if it's working or not."

He stood like a statue beside me. He was afraid too, I could tell. I wished I could hold onto his arm and tell him I knew how he felt. That I'd help if I could. "I know what you mean," I said at last. I didn't dare say the unspeakable — what if the treatments didn't work? The look in Cam's dark eyes led me to think he had the same thing on his mind.

"Do you ever feel like you've been sucked into a black hole where you can watch everybody going around like usual, only they can't see you?"

His fervent voice struck a response deep inside me. "And sometimes you hate them because it's happening to you, not them," I said slowly, and then wondered if I'd said too much.

He sighed a white cloud into the cold air and shook his head. "I'm glad it's not just me." He reached into his pocket and came out with a pack of cigarettes.

"Cam!" I said sharply. "Are you crazy?"

"It helps," he muttered, refusing to meet my eyes.

"You're crazy," I said again, after a quick silence punctuated only by the jingling of dog tags. There was no need to rub it in by asking how he thought his grandfather had gotten lung cancer.

His face went hostile, as if I had said it.

"Give me those." I grabbed the cigarettes and flung them into a snowbank. Duke went over to investigate, then calmly irrigated the spot with a stream of yellow.

"Damn it, Lori! What'd you do that for?"

I couldn't repress a wild giggle. "He knows

what's good for you." And I doubled over laughing.

Cam glanced at his watch. "I've got to go. See you around." With a brisk snap of his fingers he headed down an alley, his dog bounding at his side.

With mixed emotions I turned in the other direction.

Pancakes were sizzling on the griddle when I walked into the kitchen. I planted myself on a chair just as the espresso pot on the back burner erupted in a rush of gurgling. Mom rescued it. "How's skiing, with all the new snow?"

"Pretty good." I slid a fresh pancake off the griddle and nibbled. "Umm. Good. I'm starved."

Mom glanced at me. "Could you do me a favour and convince your brother he wants some breakfast? Even if it means inviting John."

I groaned. "Is he here?" I went upstairs and knocked on the door marked *Danger — mad scientist at work* in both English and French. Nobody answered, so I went in. Both boys were bending over Jamie's desk, which was covered with small pieces of machinery. "What's that?"

"A solar engine." John took off his glasses and wiped them with a tissue.

"He lies," Jamie muttered. "It's the ultimate weapon against snoopy sisters."

"I knocked. Breakfast time."

Jamie grunted and went back to work. His face was oddly puffy from one of the drugs he was taking, and his hair was getting quite thin. I still hadn't got used to his moth-eaten appearance.

"*Breakfast*. Mom's gonna be mad."

"I'm not hungry." Jamie scratched his head impatiently. Loose hair came away with his hand. More hair littered his shoulders.

A queasy feeling seized my stomach. "Jamie," I warned. And then I turned to John. "Want some breakfast?"

John grinned. "What're you guys having?"

"Pancakes. Probably bacon and eggs too. Mom always goes wild with breakfast on weekends."

A mischievous glint flashed in John's eyes. "I'll eat Jamie's."

"Fine," Jamie said grouchily. "Where'd you put the photovoltaic?"

But John had already left the room. Jamie mumbled some swear words and followed.

I tuned out of the breakfast table conversation and steered my pancake through the puddle of maple syrup on my plate. Derek was probably just getting up. Would he call about snowmobiling? He'd said he would, once we had a good snowfall.

Jamie got up abruptly and returned to the table wearing his down jacket.

"Jamie!" Mom was shocked. "Are you that cold? Here, let me turn up the heat."

I gulped down a swallow of orange juice. "Mom, it's roasting in here!"

Dad's eyes were puzzled behind his silver-rimmed glasses. "It does feel warmer than usual, Sheila."

"Well —" Mom was halfway out of her chair.

Jamie's teeth started chattering.

Mom reached across the bacon platter to feel his forehead. "He has a fever," she announced in a strange clipped voice. "Jim, do you think —" She got a thermometer from her odds-and-ends drawer and popped it into my brother's mouth.

"Mom!" Jamie groaned.

"Keep your mouth closed," she said tensely. "Jim, do you think I should call the doctor?"

"What?" Jamie yelped.

John and I stared at each other.

"What day of the cycle is it?" Dad asked.

Mom got up again to check the calendar. "That's it," she said. "I'd better call. Or should I try the hospital?"

"What's going on?" Jamie demanded. The thermometer fell with a clatter onto his plate.

"Take it easy, son." Dad's voice was quiet, as if everything were under control. "Do you remember the doctor explaining that one of the side-effects of your chemotherapy is a drastic reduction in the number of white blood cells?"

"Yeah." A frightened look crept into Jamie's eyes. "So I have no immunity," he muttered. He picked up the thermometer and wiped off the maple syrup. "Cripes, it's 39.5! No wonder I feel so crummy."

Mom reached for the thermometer. "These Celsius temperatures are so complicated. What's the conversion formula?"

"Multiply by 1.8, then add 32," Jamie said dully.

60

Mom was up again, fumbling for pencil and paper.

"Hang on," I said, aligning numbers in my head. "He's a little over 103."

Mom and Dad decided to forget about telephoning. Leaving their breakfast on the table, they bundled Jamie up and took him straight to the hospital. John and I sat there staring at each other over the cluttered table.

"No immunity?" John was visibly shaken. "All you'd need to do is catch a cold, and —"

There was a tense silence. I got up and started clearing the table. It felt better, having something to do.

"What will they do?" John started helping.

I thumped two mugs into the sink a little harder than I'd intended. "Dad and Jamie were talking about high-powered antibiotics once," I said slowly. "I guess they'll pump him full of those." If that didn't work, then what?

Just then the phone rang and I had to answer it. It was Derek. "Lori, have you seen all the snow?" Excitement rang in his voice and I knew he had snowmobiling on his mind.

"Yeah," I said. "I've already been out in it." I wondered suddenly whether Derek would be jealous of my chance meeting with Cam.

There was a quick pause. "You sound funny," Derek said.

I sighed. "They just took my brother to the hospital. He's got a high fever and probably no immunity."

"No immunity? How come?"

"Because of his chemotherapy. It kills white blood cells."

"Oh. Well, want to go snowmobiling?"

"Derek, I can't!"

"Why not? It'd do you good — get your mind off things."

For a moment I was tempted. I could get out of the house and away from it all. Zooming along in a sparkling sunlit world close to Derek, with the wind whipping past us, didn't sound half bad. But what if something happened to Jamie and I wasn't home? Even if Jamie were all right, my parents wouldn't be overjoyed if they came home and found a note saying I was snowmobiling. "I'd better not," I said heavily.

"Lori!" Hurt echoed in his voice. "Can't you ever let a guy have a good time?"

"Call Cam or somebody," I said. "Go anyway."

There was an abrupt silence. "Okay," he said and hung up before I even had a chance to say goodbye.

I sat down, depressed.

John was methodically carving a pancake into neat triangles. "No immunity," he muttered. "That's scary."

Did John think my brother was going to die? Quickly I got up and started running dishwater. "If they can cure cancer, they can cure a stupid fever," I mumbled. But what if that wasn't true? Then I remembered the time Jamie had shocked all of us with the news that John had had an after-death experience. I went shaky inside and grasped the edge of the sink for support. If Jamie's fever stayed up and they couldn't treat it at the hospital, the very same thing might be happening to him. I couldn't stand to think about it. Jamie gulped away by some unseen force? All of his energy gone? I picked up a plate but it slipped out of my sudsy hand and shattered.

"Oops," John said. He seemed awfully restless. "Maybe I'll go. Tell your mom thanks for breakfast. And let me know when you hear some news, okay?"

"Okay." I stood there with my hands dangling limply in the dishwater. The front door banged. And right away the house seemed very empty.

# 6
# Clearing the air

"I saw him." Heather's eyes were troubled. "They were driving down Riel Street together in his dad's pickup."

A heavy ache clamped over my chest. On the opposite side of the lab Derek and Cam were working on their chemistry experiment. Derek looked bored to death standing there while Cam wrote. And Cam looked tense.

I bent over to write too. $CuSO_4$ + Fe → $FeSO_4$ + Cu. "That slime," I said. Derek had gone snowmobiling — with Debi! — while I'd waited at home washing dishes and watching cartoons until my parents returned. Once again Jamie was in the hospital.

"I thought you'd better know."

"Thanks for telling me." Grimly I emptied the waste products out of the flask, then washed it.

Heather nudged at her glasses. "What're you going to do?"

"Kill him." I looked at the stock bottles lining the shelves. "What can we give him that'll really make him suffer? What's that red stuff?"

Heather giggled nervously. "Ask Mr. Zyschynicz."

"I know." I slapped my lab book shut. "He can have some of Jamie's medicine. That'll keep him busy throwing up. And he'll lose his hair. *And* his moustache."

The bell rang. I brushed past Derek without even looking at him, but I did catch a glimpse of Cam. He was watching me and he looked oddly guilty. So Derek had told him. It was getting harder and harder to keep my face in a proud mask as I pushed into the noisy hallway. Wendy darted past, whispering to Heather, "Guess who's waiting by your locker!"

Heather's cheeks went pink and she grabbed my arm. "Lori! Come with me! I'll die!"

I was taken aback at the excited sparkle in her blue eyes. Was it Travis Thiessen? Lately Heather had spent so much time listening to me that she'd hardly said a word about herself. "You don't want *me* around, silly!"

"Please come! I won't know what to say!"

It was so like Heather to get tongue-tied and flustered over a boy. "Relax," I coached in a low voice. "Smile. Ask if he's been skiing yet."

"When I ski like a hippopotamus?" she wailed.

"Then ask if he thinks the Oilers will beat the Canucks this weekend."

"You're hopeless!" she cried. "I don't know

which team is which. Are you talking about hockey or football?"

I hung back as she approached her locker. When Travis smiled at her, she stood absolutely still, as if everything around her had evaporated. I knew the feeling. Hating Derek, I spun the combination on somebody's locker. But when the lock clicked, ready to be opened, I drew back with a start. It was the kind of thing Jamie could do. Quickly I looked away.

Heather was ecstatic. "He invited me to a hayride his church group is having!" she whispered after he'd gone. "Lori, I'm so happy I could scream!" And then she probably thought of Derek, for a shadow crossed her face. "I'm sorry, maybe you don't —"

I went to work on her combination, which I knew. "Are you going to French without that dialogue you spent the whole weekend working on?"

She blushed again.

Derek caught up with me on the way to lunch. "What's the matter with you today?" he demanded.

I felt like elbowing him in the stomach, hard. Instead I looked at the floor. "What do you mean, what's the matter with me?"

"You've been treating me like dirt all morning." His feet slapped along beside mine in an angry rhythm.

"Well, why shouldn't I? Somebody saw you and Debi together over the weekend. With your snowmobile." My voice broke and my eyes blurred. I turned to face the wall.

66

"It was your idea. You said to call someone else."

"I suggested Cam. He doesn't happen to be female." And he's not out to get his claws into you, I wanted to add.

"Everybody else was busy."

I could tell he was lying. I took a deep breath. "This is a stupid place to have a fight."

"Okay, then let's go someplace else."

Suddenly I felt old and tired. "Let's just forget it, okay?"

For an instant hostility still flared in his eyes. Then he gave an elaborate sigh. "Sure, it's up to you."

I stepped down hard on my own foot as I moved up to the lunch counter. Perogies were the daily special, and heavy and doughy as they were, they'd fit my mood perfectly. I'd sold out instead of standing up for myself.

"The trouble is," Derek began in a more reasonable tone, "you never seem interested in me anymore."

How could he be so shallow? "I'm going through an awful lot right now, remember?" I said stiffly.

He gave a bitter laugh. "That's obvious. What're you trying to do, make everybody else suffer too?"

I nearly slapped him. "You — creep!" I turned to go but Derek caught my arm.

"I'm sorry. I shouldn't have said that."

"No kidding! For your information, Derek

Mahler, since you obviously haven't noticed, I try not to talk about it. And if I do, I try to keep it light."

"Okay, okay, I was wrong." He backed off, even though behind the counter Brenda LaCroix was ready to wait on him. "Hey, let's go someplace else so we can talk."

"Like your car?" I said dubiously.

"Like McDonald's. The drive-through. Come on, let's get out of here." He steered me out of the line. The sudden change of gears had me so unnerved I didn't know whether to stay mad or cry with relief.

The weather had turned colder. We hurried across the parking lot and settled into the comfort of car heater and stereo speakers. But we hardly spoke as we got our lunch. Derek turned up the volume on the radio, then wiggled restlessly behind the wheel. "Let's go out on the prairie."

"I don't think there's enough —" I said, glancing at my watch.

"To *hell* with school!" he exploded. "All they do is control your life — put you in meaningless compartments."

The outburst took me so much by surprise that I didn't say anything when he roared out of the parking lot. At the city limits the street narrowed by half and the cedar fences of the suburbs walled off the city so effectively it was like the end of the world. White prairie stretched endlessly, broken only by the road ahead of us, power poles, and two or three distant farmhouses.

Gravel pelted the underside of the car as Derek drove. I sank back in the seat, suddenly thinking of Jamie in the hospital. How sick was he, really? What if he didn't even make it until Christmas? The thought was so painful I bit my lip hard. The noontime sun hung lower in the southern sky than it had only a few weeks ago, and now it was flanked on either side by a brilliant glaring spot that faded above and below to form a rainbow-coloured halo. "Sundogs," I muttered.

"Yeah."

The light reflecting off ice crystals in the air meant we were in for a cold spell. Away from the protection of the city buildings the wind blew snow like sand, playing sleight-of-hands with the road. I shivered. "Slow down, Derek."

He did. But still we couldn't talk.

"Derek, I've got English. We're having a test on *Macbeth* in a couple of days and —"

"Will you relax?" he snapped. "I want to get things straightened out — unless you think your precious English is more important, and that tells me a whole lot."

I sighed and looked out across the white expanse. The car seemed a mere speck of life in a frozen desert, as if opening a window would suck away all oxygen into a void — just the way my kid brother's life could be sucked away.

At last Derek pulled over near a frozen slough. Startled Canada geese flapped into the air, honking wildly. Derek cranked down his window. "Dumb birds!" he yelled. "Don't you know there's free handouts in town?" In my mind I saw the stretch of water still open in Wascana Lake. It was always packed full of swimming geese, like an island slowly being girdled by the encroaching ice.

The crystalline air settled over me, making me want to move. "You were talking about compartments," I said cautiously. "Isn't that what our lives are anyway, most of the time?" Suddenly it was coming so clear, in terms Derek might relate to — but I was afraid of pushing it too far. "Nice, neat little packages where nothing really goes wrong. Usually you get what you want, right? Friends, nice car, spending money . . ."

"My life stinks," Derek muttered.

"*What?*" I stared at him. "What's the matter, except that a couple of friends are having their lives kicked around a little?" The familiar trembling began inside. Wouldn't I ever be able to talk about Jamie's cancer without getting shaky?

Derek avoided my eyes. "It's so bloody boring," he said. "Always the same things happening. Nobody gives a damn. I want to get out of here and try something new."

"So that's why you took Debi out," I said. Hurt ballooned inside me. "Well, if I'm so boring, just forget it." Furiously I opened the car door.

"What're you doing?" he demanded.

"Walking back." I slammed the door.

"You're nuts!" he yelled out the window. "You'll freeze."

70

"I will not."

"I didn't say *you* were boring. I just said I was bored." There was a pleading look on his face.

"Well, just take a look around you," I said sharply. "Cam's grandfather is really sick — maybe dying. And Jamie too." That just about undid me and I had to take a deep breath to keep going. "What're we supposed to do, Derek Mahler? A song and dance to keep you entertained?"

Derek swore and got out too. "I'm not blaming you," he said over the roof of the car. "It just gets old, that's all."

The wind swirled snow around my ankles. The whole situation seemed hopeless. "Let's go back," I mumbled.

"I'll be glad when I can get the hell out of here and off to Toronto for university," he muttered.

I just looked at him. University would only mean more of his compartments, but why rub it in?

"So where do we stand?" he asked when I didn't respond.

*Nowhere,* I wanted to say. It seemed that way, just the two of us talking over the roof of his car, the city in plain sight but disconnected. The only sound was the wind in my ears, the delicate hiss of snow skimming over more snow. It was as if we were stalled in a separate segment of time. I kicked at the snow. "If you're so bored, do you really want to be tied down to only me?"

"Well, we've been going around together,

after all." There was a sullen tinge in his voice. "You keep hinting that I never handle things right. How the hell am I supposed to know how if you don't tell me?"

My face flushed. I looked away. The brilliant glare of the sundogs blinded me momentarily. "You never really seem to try much," I muttered.

His fist came down on top of his car. "There you go again!"

I sighed. A pounding headache was clamping the base of my skull in a vise. On the other side of the car Derek looked as miserable as I felt.

It could never work. Things had been so good when it started, but now it seemed there were so many differences neither of us could see past them to the other person. "It's no good," I said in a tight voice. "For you or for me. If you want to go around with Debi, fine. I need more time for myself anyway." That last part wasn't true but maybe I could end up doing something worthwhile. I'd never really had to prove myself. Maybe I needed to try. After all, Jamie's situation had already begun showing me another side of life.

"So that's it? You're calling it quits?" Derek's voice was a little shaken but he didn't look exactly devastated.

"I guess so." It was hard to talk because of the lump in my throat. For an instant I wished I could take back what I'd just said. I wished I could hug him and have everything be all right between us. Even more, I wished I could take everything that had been happening over the past few weeks and put it on fast forward, like a cassette, and play the other side instead.

# 7

# Interlude

"I want to get a job," I said, standing there with a Christmas tree ornament in my hand. But there was no tree to hang it on. Mom had a thing about needlessly killing trees and Dad had a thing about artificial ones. This year they'd compromised and we were decorating the large houseplants in the living room instead.

"This is the dumbest thing I ever heard of," Jamie muttered as he draped a handful of tinsel over the jade plant.

"What? Getting a job?" These days the brat was getting so mouthy I often wanted to pound him. The blank spaces that once had been filled with Derek were driving me up a wall.

Mom laughed. "Not there, Jamie. Try the Boston fern instead."

Dad raised his eyebrows, then grinned and went back to hanging mistletoe in the doorway.

Jamie muttered something and rubbed his bald head. It was oddly shiny. He'd lost his eyebrows and eyelashes too, and sometimes he reminded me of an old-fashioned china doll. He scattered the tinsel over the hanging fern but that looked strange too. "Dumb idea," he said again. "How do you feel about all the rats and mice that were sacrificed to make sure my chemo was safe for human consumption?"

Mom's smiling mouth tightened.

"Don't you think that's a little different, son?" Dad put in mildly.

Hadn't anyone heard me? "I want to get a job," I repeated.

This time it registered. Mom's eyes widened in surprise. "What kind of job?"

"Probably something like ridding the world of all younger brothers." Jamie scowled as he dangled a plastic Santa from the philodendron.

I glared at him. "You keep out of this!" And then I turned to the cardinal in my hand. Carefully I wrapped its pipe-cleaner feet around the succulent jade branches. "Just something for after school, maybe weekends. Wendy's working, you know."

Jamie bellowed out the McDonald's song.

A spark of laughter kindled in Mom's eyes. I grinned back. "Not at McDonald's."

"*I* deserve a break today," Jamie declared. "From my MOPP. Anybody want my chemo?" He rolled a Christmas tree ball across the carpet toward the chesterfield. A black paw darted out, and then Sir Thomas Catt scampered across the floor batting the bauble ahead of him.

"Jamie!" But Mom was laughing. Ever since

Jamie had recovered from his infection she'd seemed more light-hearted.

"The daycare at the university needs someone to come in after school and help with the kids." I was still a bit uncertain because it would take all my afternoons and leave me no time for Heather. Cam had sounded interested too. It might be better to forget it and let him apply.

"You? Take care of kids?"

I turned on my brother. "It wouldn't be any different from having you in my hair all the time."

Jamie thoughtfully rubbed his bald head, then began whistling *Alouette* in a minor key. Mom winced. Suddenly I remembered the grisly words of the song. I turned on the stereo. A children's choir singing carols rang through the speakers.

Mom smiled. "Much better."

"Okay, you guys," I said. "Let's get this place Christmassy, tree or no tree. Jamie, you could climb up in the bay window and dangle the little lights so they're like stars. Mom, how would it look if we tucked the manger scene back into the plants a little? We could drape lights around the base and —"

Jamie shot me a look that was supposed to be withering. "What's the big deal, *you* running the show now?" But he boosted himself up onto the window ledge.

Mom drew in a sharp breath. "Jamie, be careful!"

"I'm not gonna fall." He sounded disgusted.

I caught Mom's eye. "If anything, he'll start swinging from the curtain rods."

Jamie made a monkey face and scratched his armpits.

Dad cleared his throat meaningfully. Mom laughed and went over to the piano where she began arranging pine cones and boughs that our Aunt Carla had sent from British Columbia — along with an awful smelling medicinal tea and some books on special diets that were supposed to cure cancer.

"About your job idea, Lori," Mom murmured, "would it leave you enough time for the things you like to do? Your skiing and running?"

"I don't know," I said helplessly. "Right now I've got too much time."

"It might not be a bad idea," Dad suggested.

"Hmm." Mom flicked a dustrag over the miniature head of Bach that sat looking down over the piano. "Have you thought about job-sharing? Then you wouldn't lose all your spare time."

It made sense. I pulled the china fawn out of a box and set it in among the plants in the window. What about Cam? He'd been acting moody lately, but any time someone spoke to him he perked right up as if nothing were wrong. Before I had a chance to back down from the idea I called him. Almost too quickly for comfort, Cam agreed.

Mom gave me a bright smile. "So the Wright boy is interested?"

"Cam Wright?" Jamie yelped. "Interested in a daycare job?"

I gave him an icy stare.

"Little boys need good role models," Dad pointed out.

"Sure — but Lori's friends? You call them normal?" Jamie howled with laughter.

"They're more normal than *you,* squirrel-brain."

Jamie gave a wild yell and leaped down from the window ledge, landing with a thud that rattled everything in the house.

"Jamie! I don't know what to do with you!" Mom bent to pick up the wreath she'd dropped at the sudden impact.

"Sorry, Mom." Suddenly Jamie was completely absorbed in looking out the window. I went to look too but saw nothing unusual — just frost crystals lining the edge of the glass pane, the snow-covered neighbourhood, the sundogs gleaming in the afternoon sky.

"Good sunlight here." Jamie was talking more to himself than the rest of us. "I bet — yeah! Those little angel chimes where you light the candles and the heat updraft — with the photovoltaic — *yeah!*" He bounded upstairs, leaving Mom, Dad and me staring at each other.

I laughed. "He sure isn't suffering."

"Obviously not. But what's he up to?" Mom's worried look had evaporated into curiosity.

Dad put his arm around her. "Maybe you don't need to worry so much. Things seem to be going well."

Mom leaned back against him. "I know, but I just can't help thinking —"

I slumped down on the chesterfield. It seemed silly and selfish to feel this way, but my parents were channelling almost all their energy into Jamie. Normally it wouldn't bother me, but I was still off-balance after breaking up with Derek.

Mom noticed my silence and came to sit beside me. "It's not easy for any of us," she said. "Lori, you're probably feeling as if your whole life is being eclipsed by Jamie's illness."

I didn't even want to try answering that one. Fortunately Sir Thomas emerged from beneath the chesterfield and settled in my lap. Automatically my hand rose to pet him. "You didn't like Derek much, did you?" I said slowly, concentrating on the cat.

Mom hesitated. "Let's just say I thought he had certain shortcomings. But I felt sure you'd outgrow him in time, so I wasn't too worried."

I sagged deeper into the chesterfield. Outgrowing Derek? That put it in a different perspective, but it still didn't help soothe the ache inside. "I think I'll go skiing," I said abruptly.

My parents didn't say a word about my walking out in the middle of the Christmas decorating. By the time I'd bundled up, Jamie came thundering downstairs talking nonstop about the angel chimes. John Duncan was coming up the front steps when I made my escape.

"It's pretty nippy for skiing," he said. "Minus twenty-six."

"I'm dressed for it." I looked past him down the street.

The chilled air shocked me out of my self pity. After all, what else could be done about Jamie's cancer? It wasn't his fault he was sick, and besides, he was making a pretty good go of it. Would I be able to face kids at school if I went bald and maybe had a death sentence hanging over my head?

The pale sunlight sifted through suspended ice crystals, giving off unexpected sparks of light as I skied. The sundogs shone so fiercely it hurt to look at them, and above the necklace-like rainbow around the sun, another upside-down arc extended until it dissolved into nothingness.

My nostrils pinched at the cold and I rewrapped my scarf so that it covered my nose and mouth. A sharp wind funnelled along the creek, swirling loose snow about my feet and numbing my face. I ducked under the footbridge, past the spot where some clown had dumped a grocery cart upside down in the creek. Now it was frozen solidly into the ice, wheels and one corner groping awkwardly toward the sky. I stopped for a moment beneath the ancient willow, where branches dangled nearly to the ice. In a patch of snow that had been undisturbed earlier in the day someone had written LORI in large letters.

I stared. Could it have been Derek? Tears trickled in icy streaks down to my scarf. Disgusted, I wiped them away. The writing probably wasn't even intended for me. Lori was a common name.

My nose began dribbling from the cold and I

shivered. It really was too bitter to stay outside for long. But before I headed back, using the tip of my ski pole, I added *SAYS HI!* after my name.

# 8
# Gathering gloom

I could tell Heather had something on her mind as we pushed through the crowded hallway at the end of the school day. It was my first day to work at the daycare centre, and since Heather could take the same bus to get home, I knew we'd probably talk it over on the way.

Someone else had come up behind me as I stood at my locker tossing books into my backpack. When I turned around, Cam was grinning down at me. "All set for diaper duty?"

I'd never thought of that aspect of the job. "*Diaper* duty?" Suddenly Heather was grinning too.

Cam's dark eyes flashed with mischief. "I had three changes yesterday. You should've seen what one of those little kids was walking around in!" He made a face and held his nose.

Heather giggled. Helplessly I joined in. "And today's my turn? Help!"

Heather patted my shoulder. "You've had babysitting experience."

I glanced up at Cam. The thought of him changing diapers seemed so absurd that I sputtered even harder. "Is it really awful?"

He shrugged and adjusted the books on his hip. "Not if you like kids. Mostly they ask you to help with the singing and crafts, and the kids all want piggyback rides."

"My brother gets piggybacks," I murmured. "But they're not rides. It's when the nurses hang an extra bag with his chemo and plug it into his IV." And then I winced. Cam's relaxed expression had frozen into a smiling mask. Hot colour flooded my face. Mortified, I glanced at Heather.

"See you around," Cam said vaguely.

"Yeah — well, we'd better catch that bus." I found I was tripping all over myself trying to make things right again. But when I tried to catch Cam's eye, he turned and walked away.

"I guess things aren't going so well for his grandfather," Heather said in a subdued voice as we boarded the bus.

Frustration burned inside me. "I could kill myself for saying that!" I said between clenched teeth. "Why didn't I *think*?"

Heather rallied to my defence. "How were you supposed to know things weren't good? At least you're being honest about the whole thing." She stared out the window and her voice went nervous. "Lori, I won't be there over the holidays — at Blefeld."

I sighed, disappointed even though I'd known it probably would come to this. But still it hurt, especially the thought of having to endure watching Derek and Debi together without Heather to turn to. "Your parents?" I asked.

"Yeah," she muttered. "It's the business about having guys there, not just girls."

"I don't know if I want to go anyway," I said dully. "I mean, with Derek and Debi — well —"

Heather gave me an embarrassed smile. The bus was pulling over at the university, so I reached for my book bag and squeezed off. And then I remembered that I still hadn't told Heather about the writing in the snow. All at once I felt completely alone as I walked along the cleared sidewalk.

I could hear the daycare centre before I could see it. Once inside, I was in a world of noisy activity and bright colours. "Hi," a frenzied looking young woman called over her shoulder. "You're Lori, right? I'm Jan. Pop into the office for a moment and then we'll be needing you in the lunchroom." She disappeared around a corner. "Jason, I *told* you —" Her voice disappeared too, masked by a loud wail.

I was tempted to disappear myself. But a few minutes later it was too late for second thoughts. There wasn't time to think of Derek. There wasn't even time to think. The room was full of tiny people wearing oversized paint shirts and smearing bright colours with huge paintbrushes.

"We're doing our Christmas decorations," Jan explained.

"Hi!" A beaming tousle-haired toddler with

orange hands and face wrapped herself around one of Jan's legs.

I took a step backwards, looking down at my school clothes.

"Hi, Kelly," Jan replied, returning the hug. "Are you done?" Then she caught my expression and shot me a wry smile. "It washes out — usually. If you'd like a paint shirt, feel free."

From that minute on I was busy mopping up spilled paint, settling arguments, wiping runny noses, and trying to keep one little boy from eating the paint. By closing time at six I was exhausted.

Jan put the last little chair on top of a table, ushered the last child and set of parents out, and gave me a tired smile. "Still all in one piece?"

Completely worn out, I looked around the bright rooms and was amazed at how they had been transformed from cheerful chaos into a quiet, peaceful setting. "I don't see how you guys do it!"

Jan pushed a strand of dark hair back from her face. "You plan like crazy and then take it as it comes, whatever it turns out to be. Last week was awful. Scott went through a biting phase and Kristi was all upset because her father had custody that week. But you get used to it."

"I hope!" I followed her out the door and wandered over to the bus stop. It was dark already. Where had the time gone? Derek hadn't crossed my mind once, nor Jamie nor Heather nor Blefeld. I was halfway tempted to call Cam to see if he'd been tired out too, but something held me back.

Our car pulled into the bus zone and there was Dad, offering me a ride home. But when we got there, things were just as hectic.

Jamie had begun his next round of chemotherapy and was lying on the chesterfield, his face sweaty and a horrible off-colour.

Mom was running around trying to fix supper and take care of Jamie, and all in a flap because someone had telephoned to inform her that she'd been selected to chair a music teachers' convention in two months. A stack of papers in need of marking sat on the counter space where she was trying to make a carrot salad. Pieces of a clarinet and a flute lay in the middle of the table.

I picked up the papers. "Want me to mark these? Or finish the salad?"

Mom gave me a surprised smile. "That would be nice. How was work?"

"Crazy." I looked at the papers in my hands. "Is this regular old math?"

"Maybe you should do the salad," Mom decided. "If Jamie weren't feeling so miserable I'd put his mechanical abilities to work. I really don't have time and this clarinet is in dire need of two screws, right when the Christmas program is coming up so soon!" She gave her hands a flustered shake and went to check on something in the microwave.

"What's the matter with the flute?" I asked, washing my hands.

"Leaky pads. I'll have to replace them tonight too, because Andrea's my best player and she has a solo in the concert. I don't know, Lori, I'm wondering whether I ought to quit my job with Jamie needing me during the day now . . ." She broke off and rubbed her temples.

She looked hassled and completely worn out. I was about to ask her if she had a headache, but the carrot slipped in my hand and I grated my knuckle instead. I winced and put it under cold water. "But you love your job, Mom."

She sighed. "There's just too much going on for one set of parents to handle. What I could use is a vacation."

Jamie was throwing up. The sound penetrated the gap in our conversation, turning my stomach. "Why isn't he upstairs?"

"He didn't have the energy to climb them," Mom said wearily, moving toward the door. "Well, I guess —"

But then Dad's calm voice came from the living room. Mom sagged and suddenly I found myself hugging her.

"Thanks, Lori," she said in a tight voice. "I don't know what I'd do without you and your father."

"Sit down, Mom," I said. "Relax a minute. Want a cup of tea? Supper can wait. I don't think anybody's starving."

"Not at the moment," she agreed ruefully. While I put the kettle on she sank down in a chair and tried a couple of scales on the flute.

There was an unnerving blank spot in the pattern of notes. "Lori, could you get my little screwdriver from my music toolbox?"

"You're supposed to be relaxing, Mom! What kind of tea do you want?"

"Earl Grey. Hand me my box of spare parts too, okay?"

"Mom!" But I knew arguing was useless. She had too much to do and she wouldn't be able to rest until her work was done.

Jamie was still on the chesterfield when I'd finished washing the dishes. "How're you feeling?" I asked as I stretched out on the floor near the stereo.

"Rotten." His voice was faint and dull.

"Anything I can get you?" The poor kid looked miserable.

He just shook his head and closed his eyes.

A pang of sympathy stabbed through me. Dad had mentioned that some of the drugs used in cancer treatment were actually poisons, administered in doses that were more lethal to the fast-growing cancer cells than to normal cells. How did Jamie feel, having to go to the hospital every few days to have his veins poked so poison could be pumped into him? I turned the stereo on softly and went to work on my algebra assignment.

Sir Thomas Catt leaped into the bay window, setting branches and Christmas ornaments swaying. I shooed him down and turned on the special lamp Jamie had set up by the angel chimes. As

the light concentrated on the solar cell, the
dangling angels began to rotate, striking their
tiny bells. All of a sudden my eyes went blurry —
poor Jamie, able to figure out all kinds of amazing things when he felt good but now so sick and
weak he could hardly lift his head.

"What's the matter with you?"

I swallowed and opened my eyes. "Nothing
important," I said.

Jamie grunted. In the kitchen the flute
sounded again, this time not missing any notes. I
stretched out flat and cradled my head in my
arms. Sir Thomas leaped over me to the window
once more, his tail thrashing back and forth as if
he were stalking prey.

*Silent night, holy night,*
*All is calm, all is bright . . .*

Startled, I lifted my head. The voices were
coming from our front yard.

"What's going on out there?" Jamie muttered.

I got up to look. A group of people stood on
our snow-packed lawn. Parked behind them on
the street was a flatbed truck loaded with bales of
hay. I flicked on the porch light to see better.
"Mom! Dad!"

They came in a hurry, probably thinking
something was wrong with Jamie. And then,
hearing the singing, they stopped short. Dad's
arm crept around Mom. She looked misty around
the eyes. Suddenly a lump clogged my throat.

Jamie muttered something that sounded impatient.

Dad opened the door. "Thank you," he said when they'd finished. Even he sounded a little choked up.

Standing safely behind him, I peered out at the group. They seemed to be mostly kids from the school choir. The city lights reflecting off the overcast sky and the snow brought every detail into sharp focus, from the grey-striped picket fence shadows slanting across the snow to the blue hockey player knitted into John Duncan's orange toque. Feet crunched momentarily on the snow; then the next carol began. An aching warmth grew inside me. As if he sensed it, Dad stepped back and put an arm around me too.

"It's pretty cold out there," Mom called briskly when they were done. "Won't you come in for hot chocolate and cookies?"

"Mom!" Jamie yelped.

I gulped. What was she trying to do, throw an instant party when we were all feeling so low?

But it was too late. Footsteps sounded on the front steps. With a knowing smile, Dad disappeared into the kitchen.

"Is it ever cold out!" the first caroller said, pulling off toque and boots and jacket.

I glanced over at Jamie but the chesterfield was empty. All I saw of my brother was his disappearing legs and feet as he crawled upstairs.

"Where's J.C.?" John's cheeks were bright red from the cold.

I pointed upstairs and pantomimed feeling sick. John nodded and threw a questioning glance in Mom's direction.

She was hustling people over toward the piano. "Why don't we have a song or two while the chocolate's heating?"

I winced. Who wanted to be herded around by an elementary school music teacher? But nobody seemed to mind. I wished I could pull a disappearing act too, but Mom glanced at me just then and gestured me over to the piano. I sighed and went. Mom played a few introductory chords and everyone started singing. Voices swelled to fill the living room. Warily I joined in.

"Here's a flute, Leanne," Mom said after *Good King Wenceslas*.

One of the grade nine girls blushed and giggled but took the flute Mom had just repaired. The silvery tone sang along through *The First Noel*.

"Hey, Mrs. C.," someone asked, "got a trumpet?"

I cringed, but Mom produced her own instrument, which she kept by the piano. By the time Dad had the hot chocolate ready, a three-piece band was playing.

I looked around for a chance to escape but John tapped my shoulder. "Think J.C.'s up to some company?"

"He feels pretty awful," I said in a guarded tone.

"Poor kid." John gestured toward the group.

"These guys don't really need me. I think I'll call it quits and go see how he's doing."

I sensed several of the kids looking at me as John went upstairs to see my brother. When I finally met their eyes, I saw pity.

It was so unsettling that I ducked away and found some privacy in the kitchen. Mom still hadn't finished marking her papers, so I sat down and went to work. It was much better than standing around knowing everybody felt sorry for me. In a way we were on display — different, apart, and everyone knew it. Cam probably felt the same way. And Jamie probably hated it most of all.

# 9
# Touch of the sundogs

On the morning of the Blefeld trip I woke up with a sore throat.

It wasn't a terrible sore throat but it was accompanied by eyes that were a little too bleary and by stuffy sinuses. I rolled over in bed and lay there on my stomach. Downstairs the telephone started ringing but I stayed where I was. I could hear Mom and Dad talking in the kitchen and knew they'd answer it.

Mom's voice prodded me out of bed. "Lori? Phone."

"Coming."

"Hi, Lori!" Wendy's greeting was bubbly with excitement. "We'll pick you up in an hour and a half, okay?"

My heart lurched. Did I dare? Now I had the perfect excuse. "Uh, Wendy —" I paused to clear my throat, hoping I wouldn't sound as guilty as I felt. "I can't go. I'm coming down with something."

"Oh, Lori!" She sounded genuinely disappointed.

Suddenly both Mom and Dad were silent. I glanced at them. Did I dare blame it on my parents? An imminent sneeze began tickling. "I know. But you know how — *aaah*" — I slapped my hand over the receiver just in time — "*CHOO!*"

"Poor kid," Wendy said. "It won't be half as much fun without you." Her voice dropped, as if she thought my parents could hear. "Maybe you'll feel better tomorrow and you can talk your mom or dad into driving you out."

"Yeah." I tried to sound hopeful.

"Well, take care of yourself. We'll miss you."

Derek wouldn't miss me. "Have a good time," I said heavily. I hung up and stood there, hardly able to believe what I'd done.

"Lori, are you sick?" Mom asked anxiously.

I joined them at the table. "I have a sore throat."

"Maybe she should stay away from Jamie," Mom said more to Dad than to me. "It's getting to be that time again."

So Jamie was vulnerable to infection again. I poured myself some orange juice even though I knew my throat would protest. "Maybe he won't get sick this time," I said. Why did they always have to think about him first?

Jamie's and John's voices came from the living room. The new home computer had been a Christmas gift to everyone, but Jamie was in his element. All he'd talked about since Christmas morning was the computer and the special computer languages he was learning. Was that all I had to look forward to for the rest of the holidays? For a moment I was tempted to call Wendy back, sore throat or no. But I didn't get up. Heather and I would find plenty of things to do together.

*    *    *

Jamie did get sick.

The commotion awakened me around five the next morning. I glanced at my clock radio, then dragged myself downstairs. I felt sluggish and achey.

"Oh, Lori," Mom said apologetically, "we didn't mean to wake you. We're taking Jamie to the hospital."

Dad was pulling on his jacket. "We'll be back after he gets settled. You'll be all right, won't you?"

"Yeah." I looked at Jamie, who was lying on the chesterfield. His cheeks were flushed and his eyes glittery with fever. He was muttering about something.

I touched his shoulder. "Hey, kid, get better, okay?"

He looked blankly at me. "Mrs. Abrams, I wasn't the one who put the mousetrap in Amy Webster's desk."

I drew back. It was spooky. My kid brother didn't even know me. "Jamie, get better," I said loudly.

Mom caught my eye. "How are you feeling, Lori?"

95

"Not so wonderful."

With swift steps she came to feel my forehead. "You're feverish too." She gave me a quick hug. "I wish we didn't have to leave you here alone. Why don't you take an aspirin and get back to bed. We'll be home as soon as we can."

I watched them go and went back upstairs. The house was unnaturally quiet. The refrigerator came on with a rattle, startling me. I lay there trying to go back to sleep. But my throat hurt. My head ached. My back ached. So I turned on my radio.

What was everyone doing at Blefeld? Were Derek and Wendy and Cam and Alan and Debi all snuggled into sleeping bags? Probably they'd be sound asleep after a day of skiing and snowmobiling. I could be too. Hot lonely tears oozed through my lashes. But it was my own fault.

Three hours later my parents still hadn't returned. I was too jittery to stay in bed, too jittery even to stay inside. So I went skiing.

The cold morning air was a shock against my hot cheeks, making my woozy internal thermostat do a few flip-flops before it decided I ought to be kept warmer than minus twenty-three. It seemed to take extra work to slide my skis over the snow, and climbing the creek dike felt like tackling Mount Everest. Once I'd reached the top I stood there, panting, dizzy, leaning on my poles.

The sun burst over the horizon, shooting shining gold and platinum into every crystal of ice. I skied toward it. Sucking in a deep breath, I angled sharply down toward the creek.

Then I lost control.

Panic churned through me. There, looming in front of me, was the grocery cart frozen upside down in the solid ice.

*Crack!*

Something snapped. I was flung forward into a twisted, tangled heap on the snow-covered ice.

But nothing happened. There was no awful, tearing pain. No blood. And nobody to help me up, nobody except Lori Carmichael who was little more than a quivering mass of nerves.

Slowly I pushed up. I ached all over, but I'd felt that way when I started out. Protruding grotesquely from the steel grocery cart basket was a broken-off segment of ski. I looked down and discovered that I was wearing the other half.

Shakily I removed my skis. I tugged at the piece stuck in the cart, but it wouldn't budge.

I looked up at the blinding light of the sundogs. Bluish purple after-images darted across my field of vision, senseless blobs that got in my way. I still felt shaky, so I sat down on the grocery cart and kicked at the piece of my ski.

I looked up the white slope to the willow, to the footbridge. Were Mom and Dad back? They'd be worried if they came home and found me gone. Home was only two blocks away, but the way I felt I might as well be walking all the way to New Brunswick.

\*　　\*　　\*

The holidays didn't improve. They got even worse when, a few days later, loud knocking at the front door jolted me out of an afternoon nap.

For a moment I lay there expecting someone else to answer. But then I remembered. Mom and Dad were both at the hospital. Jamie was still running a very high fever.

I groaned and reached for my robe. My own fever was gone, leaving in its place a miserable cold.

The knocking sounded again.

"Coming!" I yelled, although the person probably couldn't hear. If it was just a vacuum cleaner salesperson, I'd scream.

Cold air swirled around my legs as I opened the door to a tall figure, heavily bundled up. "Cam!" Suddenly I felt ridiculous, dressed in my robe and slippers. I laughed nervously. "Come on in. I'll go get something else on. I'm getting over the flu." I dressed as quickly as I could and returned to the living room.

Cam looked exhausted.

"How was Blefeld?" I asked.

"I didn't go," he said flatly.

"You didn't?"

He shook his head. "Granddad's bad off."

Confronted with something like that, words seemed pathetically useless. "I'm sorry," I said and moved over to sit beside him.

He bent forward, bracing his elbows on his knees. "The doctor thinks it won't be long now."

A pang of fear raced through me. I wished I

could touch him, offering comfort the way John Duncan had with me. "That must be so hard." My voice came out sounding brittle.

"He's just withering away," Cam said helplessly. "I never thought —" He broke off and shook his head. "Mom's at work and —"

*And you needed to talk.* But I didn't feel free enough to say it. Cam was trusting me enough to share at this very personal level and I didn't dare mess up. "Want some hot chocolate?" I asked after a nervous pause.

"Sure, okay." Listlessly he followed me into the kitchen.

My mind was spinning as I heated the milk. But finally I felt more in control. I turned to face him. "It's scary. I don't really know what to say."

He tried to shrug and smile. "Who does? It's not something that happens every day."

Impulsively I touched his arm. "Want some company going back to the hospital? Jamie's not too good either."

Cam's face went slack and he stared at me. "Jamie too? My God, I didn't know —"

"No — I mean, he's running a high temperature and he's got no immunity. It's nothing like . . ." My voice trailed off.

But the look in Cam's dark eyes let me know he understood my own fears about my brother. In so many ways he seemed years older than he had in the fall. Suddenly I wanted to hug him, to protect him in any way I could from the awful thing that was altering his life.

"You'd come with me?" He sounded uncertain.

"Of course. What're friends for?" Fear trickled through me and I knew it showed in my face, but there was no way I would back down.

He gave me an exhausted smile. "That's great, Lori."

My eyes blurred with tears but I didn't look away. Of all my friends, next to Heather, Cam Wright was the last one I'd want to be dishonest with.

The truck wouldn't start. Cam sighed and rested his head against the steering wheel. "Battery's dead."

There was so much more behind his words that a hard aching knot settled in my throat. I touched his arm. "You've got jumper cables, right? I'll get a neighbour."

A few minutes later John Duncan was self-consciously backing his mother's car down the driveway. "Hey, Lori," he said when the two vehicles sat nose-to-nose, hoods raised. "Have you seen that broken ski stuck in the grocery cart in the creek?"

Hot colour flooded my face. For an instant I relived the scary out-of-control plunge and the wrenching impact. "It's mine," I muttered, leaning against the cold truck.

John gasped and whistled between his teeth. "You really must've been travelling. The thing's wedged right in there."

"No kidding," Cam agreed. "I thought for sure they called an ambulance."

Embarrassed, I looked at the red and black cables linking the batteries of the two vehicles. "I guess I got lucky."

"You really could've hurt yourself," Cam said in a low voice. He reached in front of me, bare-handed, to check the connections. I shivered and got in the truck.

Curtains were drawn around the hospital bed when Cam and I got to his grandfather's room. The colour drained from Cam's face. He leaned hard against the wall.

I clutched at his arm. "You know how it is — they're probably just giving him a shot or something."

He pulled away and parted the curtains.

"We're trying to make him a little more comfortable," said a sympathetic nurse's voice. "Why don't you go have a cup of coffee and come back in twenty minutes."

Cam swung around, his face a stony mask. "Well, I guess we've got some time to kill."

I scuffed my toe on a dark spot on the floor. "We could go see the kid."

Cam nodded listlessly. We retraced our steps down the hallway. Loud moans echoed from one of the rooms. I winced. "Your mom works here, doesn't she?" I asked, needing to cover the awful sound.

"Yeah. Upstairs in women's surgical. I never see her much anymore because she works the three to eleven shift."

The knot was back in my throat. I'd thought

our family was hard-hit by Jamie's cancer, but Cam didn't even have someone to come home to.

We rode upstairs in a rickety elevator with a patient who looked like a wino, one eye blackened and the other bandaged. I shrank back into the corner and bumped against Cam.

Jamie was sleeping. My parents apparently had stepped out for a break. The venetian blinds were partway closed, casting stripes of shade and sunlight across my brother's face. His cheeks were flushed with fever. Blood was dripping slowly from a plastic bag suspended on the IV pole. Jamie stirred in his sleep, setting the whole intravenous apparatus jiggling. I clenched my jaw but a few tears spilled anyway.

Cam nudged me. He was holding the box of tissues from Jamie's bedside stand.

I blew my nose. "I should leave him a note," I said, determined not to turn into a soggy mess.

*Hi, kid,* I wrote on a paper towel. *Came to see you but you were sleeping. Are they nuts letting you sleep till four in the afternoon? When are you coming home to figure out how to break into the school's computer? Your ever-loving sister, B.F. P.S. Since when have you been on the vampire diet?*

Cam was looking over my shoulder. "B.F.?"

I grinned. "Buffalo face. For some reason, he thinks that's my name."

"He's nuts. Can't he appreciate the local scenery?"

Something sparked inside me and I shot Cam

a teasing glance. "Are you implying that I look like the prairie?"

He smiled. "No, I was thinking of those Richardson's gophers."

"Thanks a lot!" I tried giving him a shove, but of course he didn't even sway.

Instead he caught my hand and the moment of fun evaporated. "I want to get back to Granddad," he said in a tense voice.

I squeezed his hand gently. Suddenly he was holding on as if I were a lifeline. I took a long look at Jamie as we left.

Four silent old men lay there as Cam and I walked in. At first I didn't even recognize Cam's grandfather. He had the pathetic look of a famine victim, skin sallow and transparent with illness, eyes huge and staring with suffering in a face so emaciated it was almost skull-like. I bit down hard on my lip as Cam sat on the bed and reached for the old man's bony hand.

Cam bent forward. "How're you feeling, Granddad?"

The old man's dark eyes focused on me and he extended his free hand. I took it. It was cold.

"You look like a nice young lady," he said in a faint whisper.

"You know Lori." Cam sounded embarrassed. "You've met her before."

Cam's grandfather gave my hand a feeble squeeze. "Do me a favour, Lori." I nodded and waited for him to continue. He seemed to be drifting, almost as if he'd forgotten he was about to say something. And then he looked directly at me once more. "Get this character here to throw away his cigarettes. I'd sure hate to have him learn the hard way, like I did."

I glanced at Cam out of the corner of my eye. He had turned a miserable dull red. I pretended not to notice and looked back at the old man. "I'll try," I said awkwardly.

"Good." He went into a weak spasm of coughing.

Cam didn't speak. So I turned to him. "I'd better go," I said. It was too scary — too private. I didn't belong. Cam's grandfather was still coughing, but it wasn't much more than a wheeze.

"Here's the suction, Granddad." Cam placed the end of a piece of tubing in his grandfather's mouth. There was a horrendous gurgling sound. I didn't look at what came out.

Shaken, I backed away. "See you later," I said.

Cam looked up at me. "Lori, I'll drive —"

"No, that's okay. I'll take a bus."

But before I finished Cam had his hand raised, shushing me. For a long silent moment he sat there, poised, rigid with tension. And then, finally, he relaxed with a sigh. "It's okay. He's just fallen asleep." Gently he pulled a blanket over his grandfather. "All day he's been talking about feeling hot, but if you touch him he's cold. It scares me. Usually it's the other way around."

The ache in my throat grew tighter. It was almost too much to handle. On another floor

Jamie was very sick — though obviously not as ill as the old man. What really undid me was seeing the tender way Cam cared for his grandfather.

Cam was looking out the window, past the other three patients in the room. He looked so tired. Any traces of hope seemed to have disappeared.

I sat down beside him on the bed, slipping my arm around him. He sighed and pulled me closer. We didn't speak.

Twenty minutes later nothing had changed. Except for the way his arm rested around my shoulder, Cam hardly seemed to know I was there. And I was getting incredibly fidgety. I mumbled something about checking on Jamie and Cam let me go.

My brother was awake but his head was thrashing back and forth with fever. Mom sat tight-lipped in a chair, while Dad leaned against the sink reading the newspaper.

"Is his temperature really high?" I whispered.

"They're getting ice packs." Mom's eyes were weary. "It's good of you to come, Lori."

"Cam brought me," I mumbled. What if Jamie began withering away like Cam's grandfather and we lost him? A cold terror gripped me. It was possible. "Isn't the antibiotic working?" I asked, talking to push away the horrible thoughts.

Dad shook his head with the faintest motion.

"They haven't been able to identify the virus yet. They just took more cultures."

"Why was he getting blood earlier?" I asked.

Dad was smoothing his beard, which was not a good sign. "The doctor thought it might help — extra white cells to fight the infection."

I looked back at Jamie. For an instant I saw the bony sunken face of Cam's grandfather superimposed on my brother's body. I shuddered and squeezed the back of a chair. I squeezed it so hard it creaked.

"Are you all right, Lori?" Mom asked. "You look so pale." She turned to Dad. "Take her home, Jim, so she can get some rest. The poor girl is still half sick herself. I'll be all right. I'll spend the night unless Jamie's fever breaks."

I nodded and stumbled woodenly down the hall. People were sick, dying, and there was nothing I could do to change it, or even help. Instead I got sent home. What kind of world was it anyway?

Many hours later the telephone rang, jangling me out of a sleepless stupor. I staggered out of bed.

The ringing stopped. Dad appeared at the foot of the stairs. "I wish you'd ask your friends not to call in the middle of the night," he said irritably.

Something was wrong. I knew it. I nearly tripped on my way downstairs.

It was Cam. "He died," he said in a stunned, broken voice. "Can you work for me next week?"

"Oh, Cam!" I bit my lip and sagged as shock drained away the strength in my legs. In the pained silence I could hear blood rushing in my ears. "Can I help?"

"Just show up at work. Will you?"

"Of course! Cam, I —"

"Thanks." The telephone clicked.

I stared at the receiver. In the background I could hear the late night jazz show Dad always listened to. I wandered into the living room. Dad lay on the chesterfield with stacks of books and psychology journals on the floor beside him.

An awful aching emptiness filled me. And then Dad looked up, meeting my eyes. "What's wrong, Lori?"

I stumbled across the room to rest my head against him. "Cam's grandfather died."

His arms came around me.

"He was so sick and there was nothing I could do for him or Cam, and Jamie's so sick and —" I couldn't go on.

There was a brief silence. "It makes us feel pretty helpless," Dad agreed after a moment. And I was sure I wasn't just imagining the pain in his voice.

# 10
# Making contact

"Where's that Wright keeping himself?" Derek demanded irritably as we all sat around a lunch table the first day back at school. "He cops out on Blefeld and never says a word, and now school too! I didn't have a lab partner in chem."

There was no awkward silence, no accusing look directed at Derek. Uneasiness crept through me. The others obviously didn't know.

Alan laughed. "He picked a good day to skip. We had a sub in English and she made us read aloud just to kill time."

"Maybe he's sick." Wendy sounded concerned.

I took a deep breath — might as well come right out with it. "His grandfather died."

They were shocked.

Wendy was the first to respond. "I thought he'd get better," she said wistfully. "I mean, Jamie's doing so well."

It was obvious that nobody else knew what to say. "I guess it doesn't always work out that way," I said heavily.

"Everybody gets hard breaks sometimes." The thoughtful tone in Debi's voice surprised me. But maybe she'd know, after having several step-fathers and a mother who never really settled down.

"He'll handle it," Derek said confidently. "He's a trooper, just like Lori here. Anyway, old people die. So what else is new?"

A french fry dropped from my hand into my glass of water. "Derek Mahler! How can you be so — so unfeeling? Cam just lost the only person who's ever been like a father to him."

It was almost satisfying to watch the mottled red creeping up Derek's neck. I decided to press my advantage. "How would you feel if your dad died?"

He looked away. "Kinda numb, I guess."

"You're just naturally numb anyway," I muttered, staring hard at a ketchup spot on my napkin. "You'd think with a doctor for a father you'd have more sympathy for other people." And then I wished I hadn't said it. Any good feelings I'd had toward Derek were gone. There was no point in turning the rest into a feud.

The table jiggled. "I wish people would quit comparing me to my old man!" Derek practically yelled.

Debi got up. "Come on, Derek, let's go."

Shamefaced, I glanced at Wendy and Alan.

"He had it coming," Alan said with a sympathetic smile.

I gritted my teeth.

The rest of the day degenerated into an oddly guilt-stricken ordeal. Nobody seemed to want to talk about Cam — and I probably felt the worst of all. Even though Jamie was still in hospital battling his high fever, at least he was alive. Cam's grandfather wasn't and nothing could change that.

It was a relief to get to the daycare centre after school. The minute I stepped through the door a shrieking blonde child threw herself at me in a flying hug.

I scooped her up and brushed her soft hair back from her eyes. "How are you, Sarah? Did Santa bring you lots of presents?"

The little girl looked solemnly at me. "Scott bited me," she announced, pointing to a bruise on her arm. "He sitted in the corner and didn't get his snack till last."

I eased her down and we walked hand in hand into the noisy playroom. As always there was activity everywhere. Amy and Jessica and Tara were running around with coloured scarves fluttering behind them. Scott and Adam were climbing up the indoor slide, while Nathan sat at the top, shouting at them to get out of his way. Kristi and Jason sat side by side on the battered old chesterfield looking at books.

I sighed with relief. The children were so busy being themselves. They were untouched by issues like illness and death.

Melissa noticed me and tore across the room. "Lori! Carry me upside down!"

I grinned. She obviously remembered the time I'd stood her on her head. "Okay, but just once," I said. Otherwise I'd be mobbed with kids asking for endless turns.

The little girl stomped her foot. "Eleventy-three times."

"Once." I swung her upside down and she shrieked and giggled so loudly several other children came running over.

*"Superman!"*

The cry distracted me. Christopher, apparently tired of the congestion on the slide, leaped off the platform where he'd been waiting behind Nathan.

The scream and bloody nose that followed kept Jan and me busy for a good ten minutes. Then tiny Megan had to be changed.

"Whew!" Jan said when she got a chance. "Will it ever end?"

I grinned and brushed my hair out of my eyes. "Nope." I didn't want it to either. It was far better than school and watching the others trying to deal with the sad news.

Jan patted Eric's curly head. "What we could use right now is Cam and his guitar. He can grab their attention and settle them down just like that."

"He plays guitar?" To cover my surprise I picked up a used tissue off the floor and shot it into the wastebasket.

"Does he ever. He does the best *Old MacDonald* I've ever heard."

"Andrea," I called, "the record player is only for grown-ups to use." And then 1 noticed Scott lurking under the table, eyeing the plug to the record player. Quickly I ushered the little boy to a vacant tricycle.

Jan was setting out construction paper and scissors. "That one scares me," she said, shaking her head. "I'm afraid he's really going to hurt himself one of these days. But you should see him with Cam around — he quiets right down."

"I wish I could see him working here," I said wistfully.

Jan grinned. "You'll get a chance, don't worry. Valentine's Day is a big party day and all the staff are supposed to come."

Everything felt more back to normal by closing time. But Dad wasn't waiting for me. After ten minutes I caught a bus, wondering if anyone would be home.

The lights were on as I came up the front walk.

"Hello?" Mom called.

I moved into light and warmth and the smell of lasagna. "Dad never picked me up."

Mom shot me a quick sympathetic smile. "He just phoned. One of his grad students is having an impossible time with the statistics for her thesis." She washed her hands. "I thought we'd go ahead and eat supper, just the two of us. Dad can eat whenever he gets home."

I helped her set the last of the food on the table. "How's Jamie? How come you're not at the hospital?"

Mom smiled and a lot of the tension slipped out of her face. "His fever broke and he's sleeping quietly. You've had so little home life lately I thought it would be nice to be here together." She turned on the classical radio station and sat down.

The lasagna was delicious, much better than the TV dinners I'd been throwing in the oven every night. But halfway through my first helping I paused as an idea jangled through me like a bolt of electricity. "Mom, could we have Cam over for supper sometime?" I asked hesitantly. "His mom works nights and he's got nobody at home now."

"The poor boy! Yes, of course!"

I bit my lip. Compared to most of the guys I knew, Cam didn't seem much like a boy anymore.

Mom's eyes were gentle on me. "You've done a lot of hard growing up this year, haven't you? We've had to be so involved with Jamie that I feel horribly out of touch with what's been happening in your life — for example, your accident with your skis."

Suddenly self-conscious, I gulped down another mouthful of salad. "I went skiing. I lost control and my ski broke. You know I didn't get hurt."

Mom sighed and rubbed her eyes.

"Don't you want to go see Jamie again tonight?" I asked. "I'll be okay." Not that I wanted to stay by myself.

"Jamie's in good hands," Mom said firmly. "Right now I'm concerned about you."

I wished I could spill it out to her, how breaking my ski seemed like a symbol for everything else that seemed to be happening in my life. How I didn't feel right around my friends anymore, except Heather, and now she was busy with Travis a lot of the time. How sometimes I felt as if I didn't even know myself. How sometimes I seemed to be walking a tightrope across a deep gorge, watching other people fall into that gorge. People like Cam's grandfather. Like Jamie.

I let my chin drop into my hands. "I don't understand things anymore," I muttered. "Things that used to be important just seem — dumb."

Mom sighed again. "Lori, I know the feeling. But we'll just have to have faith that everything will work out. Things usually do." She paused, then went on. "I'm leaving my job for the rest of the year," she said more briskly. "All except the music classes, which will be more than enough with that convention next month."

"You're *what?*" A curious flat emptiness enveloped me, even though Mom had mentioned the possibility once before. "Won't you go nuts with all that extra time?"

"I need to be here for Jamie," she said. "And for you too, I think."

We ate silently for several minutes. Then Mom smiled at me. "Is there anything you'd like to do this evening?"

A panicky on-the-spot feeling washed through me. Was that how Jamie felt when Mom fussed over him too much? "I've got some home-work," I said guardedly. "But maybe we could play some gin rummy or something." The evening turned into a quiet oasis between times of fear and pain.

*       *       *

The funeral for Cam's grandfather was held two days later. The church was much too large for the number of people present. We all sat together — except for Derek and Debi, who never showed up.

I fell apart when Cam and his mother and older married sister followed the casket out of the church. There was a stoniness in Cam's face that was so alien to the person who'd been carefree and easygoing only a few months before.

"It's all right," Heather whispered, squeezing my shoulder.

"Are you going over to the house?" Wendy whispered behind me as we walked past the coffin at the snowy gravesite, each of us sprinkling a handful of fresh earth on the casket.

"I don't know," I said helplessly. "What's it supposed to be, a reception?" The idea seemed revolting, too much like a party. But how would Cam feel if none of us came?

"Come on, ride over with me," Wendy begged. "Heather's got Travis and Alan brought his car."

So I went with Wendy and we nibbled at finger-sized sandwiches and talked politely with adults we'd never met before. Cam was holding himself aloof, sitting silently on a chesterfield between two relatives who were talking non-stop.

"We ought to rescue him," Alan said.

"How?" Last fall it would've seemed easy. But now so many things had changed. Did Cam even want to be rescued?

As the three of us stood there in our Sunday best, an awful feeling washed through me. The next reception like this could be for Jamie, in our house. How could I ever stand it?

I sensed Cam watching us. I swallowed hard as he walked across the room to join us. And then the four of us were standing there, not knowing what to say.

It was Wendy who broke the ice, giving Cam an impulsive hug. Then Cam reached for me too and the three of us stood there, linked. "Oh, hell," Alan muttered and threw his arm around Wendy. We kept on standing there, all four of us caught by emotions we couldn't talk about.

# 11
# Rough ice

Cam's and Heather's birthdays were two days apart. Somebody — probably Wendy — decided it was time for a change of gears and the result was an evening barbecue and skating party at the lake.

It was held on Cam's birthday, which was my day to work. I couldn't help feeling nervous and impatient as closing time came and little Kristi still hadn't been picked up. Scraps of construction paper, bread crusts and crayon tips scooted ahead of the broom as I swept. "Kristi," I said to the dejected little girl, "want to hold the dust pan for me?"

Slowly she got up. "I'm always last when Daddy has me."

She looked so worn out it tugged at something inside me. It couldn't be easy staying one week with one parent and the next with the other. Impulsively I bent down and kissed her forehead. "Your daddy loves you," I said. "He's just so busy it's hard for him to get away from his office."

Kristi wrapped her arms around my legs and hung on. At that moment Heather and Travis walked in. "Ready?"

"Are you going too?" Kristi asked pathetically.

I gave up on the sweeping and sat down in one of the tiny chairs, holding her on my lap. "I'm not going *anywhere,* Kristi, until your daddy comes."

Heather was radiant in her new contact lenses, a birthday present from her parents. "It doesn't matter if we're a little late. Parties never get started on time anyhow."

"Is my daddy coming?" Kristi asked wistfully. Then her face crumpled. "I want Mommy."

I rocked her, stroking her wispy hair. "Her parents have joint custody," I explained to Heather. "This is her dad's week."

"How awful." Heather mouthed the words.

"It's life." I took a deep breath and asked the question that had been on my mind all day. "Is Cam going to the party?"

"Of course! He and Alan were talking about it on the way to algebra."

Relief spun through me in a giddy wave.

"He's been staring at you again," Heather whispered with a teasing sparkle in her blue eyes.

I could feel the extra pink creeping into my cheeks. "He has not. Every time I look at him he's looking somewhere else."

Heather giggled. "He's careful. It's a scream watching him!"

*"Daddy!"*

The ecstatic shriek brought me to my senses. Kristi was thrust high into the air, then enveloped in a bear hug.

I cleared my throat. "Uh — Mr. Morris?" It was hard to sound bossy with a lawyer. "The centre closed fifteen minutes ago and Kristi's been awfully worried —"

"Sorry I'm late, sweetie," he said without even glancing my way. He planted a kiss on the little girl's cheek. "Shall we go to McDonald's? And then I have a surprise waiting for you at the house." The man ushered his young daughter out the door.

Heather stared after them. "He acts like he owns the whole world!"

I grimaced. "Some people are like that." I began setting chairs on top of the tables. Heather quickly moved to help.

"You know," she said suddenly, "I just can't see Cam working here."

"I can. And everybody says he's fantastic with the kids." I reached for my skating gear. "I'm all set."

The evening was crisp and not too cold. Music came through the public address system at the lake and the bonfire sent flames leaping up to meet the darkness while figures glided over the ice. Anticipation danced through me.

"What kept you guys?" Wendy called from a bench where she sat lacing up her skates.

"A late father," I yelled back.

Blades clashed against ice as Alan and Cam skated over.

"Slowpokes!" Alan teased. "We just about barbecued without you!"

Cam's dark eyes met mine for an instant. "Kristi's dad?"

I nodded. "The poor kid was so upset."

"Can't say I blame her — three years old and tossed back and forth like a frisbee." Before I had a chance to reply he was off again with long, sure strokes. Ever since the funeral he had seemed more like himself. "Hey, Murphy! Let's check out the island and find a table."

I sat down with Heather to put on my skates. "Those guys! All they ever think about is their stomachs!"

"Not that one." Heather giggled, pointing. On a bench nearby Derek and Debi were kissing, oblivious of us.

"Two things, then." I tied my laces and pushed off. The ice was pitted. I went into an experimental glide but the bumpy surface slowed me down, holding me back. "Crummy ice!" I called to Wendy who was trying out a figure eight.

"Show-offs!" Heather said from the bench.

I smiled as Travis took her hand and they skated cautiously toward the island.

"Come on!" Wendy beckoned impatiently. "It's better out here."

I followed her. The surface was better farther from the shore and I was able to lose myself in the gliding motion, the wind whooshing gently past and my skates humming over the ice.

"Not bad, eh?" Wendy called.

"Not bad." I looked back over my shoulder and leaned into a lazy curve.

"Hey, lady! Better watch where you're going!"

Cam and I were headed for the exact same spot. I gasped and swerved. He caught my arm. For a second or two we hovered off balance. Then, still holding on, he pushed off with powerful strokes. I looked at him in surprise, then matched his rhythm. It was effortless. It was like flying, a heady feeling of aliveness as the rest of the world swept by in quick flashes. I didn't even need to worry about where I was going because Cam was steering for both of us. It was utter freedom, something I'd rarely felt since Jamie became ill.

All too soon it was over. Grinning, Cam deposited me at a picnic table on the island. Alan was busy lighting the coals.

"Happy birthday!" I gasped.

Cam's dark eyes sparkled with fun. "You liked the ride?"

The wild, free feeling lingered. "Do I get another turn?"

"Actually, I brought you over to cook the steaks."

"Cam!" I stuck my tongue out at him.

A devilish glint flashed in his eyes and he was off again. A moment later he reappeared with a very flustered Wendy.

"Cam Wright!" she sputtered. "Why'd you let me fall? Now my whole backside's out of joint!"

"Should've brought a pillow," he retorted. "And *I* should've brought my camera." He turned to me with a slow wink and took off once again.

Wendy swivelled around, twisting first one way and then another, brushing off the seat of her pants. "I'm crippled for life," she moaned. "That silly knucklehead!"

I grinned. "Need a wheelchair?" Fragments of the exhilarating ride still drifted dreamlike around me. Not once had there been the slightest fear that Cam would let me fall.

After eating, we sat around the coals making toasts with our hot apple cider.

"To the birthday kids," Wendy said.

"To birthdays!" Cam added.

The styrofoam cups didn't make any noise.

"These things don't exactly clink," Alan said.

Wendy shot him a dirty look. "To glasses that clink, then! If you don't like these, you bring them next time."

"To friends," I said.

There was a quick hush. "To *girl*friends," Derek added, smiling at Debi.

Cam stood up. "Hey! Since I'm the birthday boy, don't I get to kiss all the girls?"

"Are you kidding?" Wendy retorted. "After you dumped me on the ice?"

"Step right up," Cam said. And since no one did, he reached for Debi's hand. "Allow me."

An odd streak of jealousy twisted through me.

"Hey!" Derek protested. "What do you think you're doing, Wright?"

"Fair's fair," Cam said with a wicked grin. Leading Debi by the hand, he skated off with her.

I felt sick.

But they were back a moment later. "Next?" he called. Since nobody got up, he turned to Wendy.

"No way!" she yelped.

Laughing, he pried her up from the bench.

I dug my skates into the snow and wished I were at home. Then I reminded myself that it was just a game, after all. And besides, I had no special claim on Cam Wright.

Soon they were back and Cam was holding out his mittened hand to me. For some reason I went weak in the knees. "Hey, Wendy," I said to cover my nervousness. "Did he dump you again?"

She shook her head. "I should've dumped him. Want to do me the favour?"

"Want to skate a little?" Cam asked as we stepped onto the ice. A crooked grin flashed across his face.

I felt a smile welling up inside. "Sure!"

We took off with the same sweeping strokes and right away we were flying. Laughter burst out of me. "I haven't had this much fun in ages!"

"Me neither," he said in a low voice.

I wanted to skate like that forever. But then one of my skates caught in a crack in the ice. I flew forward. Memories of skiing into the grocery cart slammed through me and I cried out. But I didn't fall.

"Hey!" Cam steadied me. "That was close!"

I clung to his arm. "That scared me!" I gasped.

"You're shaking! Are you all right?"

Since my legs didn't want to hold me up, I sat down on the ice. "I was thinking about the other time," I said. "When I broke my ski."

"Oh." Understanding flickered in his dark eyes and he sat down beside me.

We sat there silently for several minutes. When I pushed off at last, I understood how Heather felt on the ice. The trembly feeling still hadn't gone and even the simplest glide was tense and jerky.

"Relax," Cam said. "It won't happen again."

"I can't." My teeth started chattering. My feet were so cold they were achey-numb.

"Take it easy," he said, matching my slow pace.

"How's everything going?" I asked a few minutes later.

He pulled back. "Fine."

It was obvious he didn't want to talk anymore, so I didn't even try.

"The worst is over."

I nodded and bit my lip, wondering what had happened to the feeling of closeness that had sprung up between us only a few weeks ago. There was no point in making things even more awkward by asking if he wanted to come over for supper sometime — or by asking if he'd quit smoking, although I hadn't seen him with a cigarette all evening.

124

But then he relaxed. "You're the one with the tough assignment," he said quietly. "I'd never trade places with you. Not a chance."

"Jamie's out of the hospital now." My voice felt stiff. The infection had lasted two weeks — and he could easily have another with each cycle of chemotherapy. The way the doctors explained it, the infections could be more deadly than the Hodgkin's disease.

The others whooped and laughed as we skated back.

"Things really got hot, eh?" Alan yelled. "You guys were gone half an hour!"

Wendy elbowed him in the ribs. "Only fifteen minutes, you dope."

Startled, Cam and I glanced at each other. Then he began to laugh. "I forgot! We were skating — and talking."

"Uh-huh."

"Sure."

"Right. Talking without words, I bet."

"No, honest!" And then he grinned down at me. "Can't pass up the chance."

In a daze I watched as he bent toward me. His nose bumped against mine. It was cold. Then his lips touched mine in a soft, gentle kiss. The breath drained out of me. I wanted to reach out to him, asking for more, but we were right in front of everybody.

Cam backed off. "Next?" Compared to before, his voice was subdued and oddly husky.

Heather blushed and scooted closer to Travis.

Alan grinned. "Do I get a turn now?"

"*Forget it!* Give it up, guys, will you?" Wendy's protest cut through the clearest.

"What do you think we are?" I added. "A bunch of brainless —"

Derek snickered.

"I'm sorry," Cam said at the same moment. "It's my fault. I started it."

Right away the tone of the evening changed. Derek and Debi disappeared. Cam and Alan and Wendy went back onto the ice. I sat there on the bench wishing I'd kept my mouth shut — except if things had kept going on that way everybody would've felt bad afterwards.

I gave Cam one last lingering look across the ice when Heather and Travis offered me a ride home. Maybe it was absurd to let myself be carried away by the feelings that were stirring inside. Maybe there were too many differences, despite what we'd both been going through.

As soon as I stepped inside the house I could hear my brother's voice murmuring along with what sounded like a video game. "There goes the Incredible Hunk — and Lori's after him. Oops! She's got him cornered — *BAM!*" A thunderous explosion sounded on the TV set.

Hurt rage churned through me. I slipped around the corner to watch. Two tiny figures were making their way through a TV maze. My brother's fingers were busy on the computer keyboard. "There goes the Hunk again. Here she comes, and — *KA* —" He looked up just as the figures exploded.

I felt like slapping him across the face. Instead I yanked out the cord. The TV went blank.

"Didn't like my game, eh?" A challenge flashed in Jamie's face, just waiting for me to snap back at him.

"No." I took a deep breath and sat down on the floor. "You really got the TV to do that?"

"Sure. It's easy. You punch in the right data and you've got the maze. You make your drawings on a grid and punch in the sums of your co-ordinates and there's the people and —"

"Great, Jamie, just great," I said with a sigh.

My brother looked deflated, as if he'd really wanted me to screech at him.

I got up and headed upstairs. Maybe control was the name of the game. Little Kristi had been working on that one, waiting for her father. It might help with some of my problems too. Things like being scared silly by almost falling. Like standing up for what was right with my friends — and not letting my kid brother get the best of me. Maybe it was worth a try.

# 12
# Game over?

Hoarfrost etched every branch and power line with white as Heather and I walked home along the creek. When we got to the huge willow by the footbridge I reached for a dangling branch. The fluffy white sat so delicately on my mitt that I couldn't feel a thing.

"You never talk about skiing anymore," Heather said. "Or skating, or running, or even Cam. What's wrong?"

I hesitated. If I couldn't talk to Heather about these things, who *could* I tell? "I'm trying to keep everything under control," I said at last. It came out sounding grim. I kicked at a chunk of snow.

Heather sighed. "Lori, you've got to relax and have a little fun."

"We could do aerobics at my house."

"That's not what I mean!" she said impatiently. "You're starting to act like a tired old lady."

"I can't help it!" I said, wounded. "Anyway, I'm going to the movie tonight with the others."

Heather sighed again. "I didn't mean to make you feel bad."

"Come to the movie." Suddenly I was pleading with her. Sometimes she felt like my only link with the group, but ever since Travis had come into the picture she'd been spending less and less time with the rest of us.

"You know how Travis feels about monster movies." With her mittened hand she brushed wisps of hair back from her face.

"I have fun at the daycare centre," I said, getting a better hold on myself. "Probably it's just burnout. Too much stress and everything."

"You ought to know, with a psychologist in the family."

There was a trace of bitterness in my laugh. "He spends all his time on Jamie. And his teaching." And Jamie was turning into a cheeky brat, talking back all the time and expecting service at the snap of a finger. But how could I tell Heather these things without sounding full of self-pity?

Heather shifted her books to her other arm, then pointed. "Hey! What's that?"

I looked. There it was again, *LORI* written in the soft snow on the creek bank.

"Uh-oh! You've got a secret admirer!" There was a teasing lilt in Heather's voice. "I bet it's Cam. He's always watching you, you know."

I didn't want to think about him. These days Cam Wright walked around campus joking and laughing as if his grandfather had never even been sick. He'd broken through the cloud and I hadn't. Jamie was still sick. And Jamie was still Jamie, getting worse by the minute.

"I bet it is," Heather persisted.

"There must be five Loris just in this neighbourhood," I muttered. "Probably some grade six kid wrote her own name to convince the world that somebody's madly in love with her."

Heather gave my shoulder a little shake. "Quit being so cynical."

I didn't say anything. How could I help feeling that way when so many things kept going wrong? I snapped a dead branch off the willow. A white cloud of hoarfrost drifted down around me. After *LORI* I wrote *WHO?*

"Let me see that." Heather reached for the stick and began tracing out *TRAVIS*.

I sat there on the grocery cart kicking at my ski. But the dreamy look on Heather's face was too tempting. I dumped a handful of soft snow on her.

"Oooh!" she sputtered. "You're hopeless!" She got me in return and ran, giggling.

I chased after her but my steps slowed. Silently we walked to my house.

The house was spotless. It was too spotless, except for the coffee table where Jamie and John were working on something.

Heather bent over to look. "What're you guys up to?"

Jamie went right on whistling *Alouette* in a minor key.

For an instant I felt like banging my books

down on his bald head. The whole thing was getting pretty stale.

But John looked up, brushing a hand through his hair. "Ever hear of a solar powered pencil sharpener?"

"A what?" There among the other mechanical parts was our big pencil sharpener, removed from the wall.

John grinned. "It'll be the world's first. Think we can make some bucks off it?"

"Well —" I turned to Jamie. "Does Mom know you took it down?"

He still didn't look up. "What's she need it for anymore? All she does all day is bug me and worry about that stupid music convention."

Heather was shifting her weight from one foot to the other. "Maybe I should go," she hedged. "I've got all that algebra . . ."

I shot her a pleading look. "I could help you. Let's have a Coke and then get to work."

But she didn't set her books down. "I never understand it unless I work everything out for myself."

"Stick around and we'll sharpen your pencils," John offered.

Jamie scowled. "We'll practice on Lori's fingers."

"You will not!" I glared at him. "How come you have to be such a little brat, just because you feel so sorry for yourself?"

Jamie stood up, knocking against the coffee table. Tools and pieces of the gadget jiggled. "You think I *like* feeling crummy all the time? Why don't you go take my shots next time and see how *you* like it. Damn MOPP."

"I wouldn't like it," I muttered. I glanced at Heather. She looked awfully nervous.

"How would you like going to school with no hair or eyebrows or eyelashes and hearing kids making cracks behind your back?" Jamie's face was reddening and his eyes were bright and bitter. "How would you like dreaming you're gonna die — and waking up and knowing it could happen? Want my cancer? You can *have* it!" He kicked the coffee table again and again until it tipped over.

"I've got to go." Heather walked out before I could stop her.

"Jamie!" Mom stood in the doorway, her brown eyes blazing. "You go to your room this minute!"

"Aren't you going to make him clean up?" I cried, pointing. "Just look!"

"Can't make me," Jamie taunted. He wandered over to the piano and banged out a two-fingered version of *Chopsticks*. "Piano's out of tune, Mom."

"How would you know?" I demanded. "Have you got perfect pitch?"

"I might." He shot me an insolent look. "Mom, go get your piano tuning stuff. Think I can do it as well as you?"

"*James Carmichael!*" Mom was nearly shrieking. "If you weren't so — I ought to spank you!"

"Do it!" I cried. "You should've done it three weeks ago!"

Mom looked ready to blow a fuse. Tight-lipped, she left the room, muttering something about why wasn't Dad around.

Jamie climbed up on the swivel piano stool. "Because he's up in his ivory tower." Then he jumped, knocking the stool over too.

Moving like a stocky bull terrier, John grabbed my brother's arm. "Will you quit being such a pain in the ass? The world wasn't made just for you."

"Shove it, Duncan." Jamie brushed past and bundled into his jacket. "See ya later."

John and I stared at each other. His eyes were full of pain. I was just about ready to cry. In the kitchen I could hear Mom babbling hysterically into the telephone. I picked up the piano stool, then helped John with the coffee table. Piece by piece we collected bits of equipment off the carpet.

"It's that time of year," John said at last. "Everybody's going bonkers. Stir crazy."

The winter was so long and cold, even though subtle changes in the January sunlight made it clear that spring would be here eventually — maybe in another three or four months. In the meantime we had all of February and March to endure. And in just a few hours I'd be out with the other kids trying to pretend nothing was wrong. It was that or stay home with the brat.

\*　　\*　　\*

A few hours later the smell of pizza filled the air. We were all squeezed onto benches at a table. Heather wasn't there. I was squished in next to Wendy, just the way it had been at the theatre — between Wendy and the aisle.

Derek reached for another slice of pizza. Long strings of melted cheese stretched down to the metal serving plate.

"Watch out!" Debi laughed and tugged at the strands, popping what broke off into her mouth. "Umm!" There was a new softness in her face that almost made her pretty, no longer a vinyl mask of perfection. It took no guessing to figure out the change.

"Wasn't that monster something else?" Wendy said with a giggle. She shuddered. "He looked so *real*. And all that slime — yuck!"

"Oozing out of the black swamp waters," Alan said dramatically.

Across from me Cam grinned. "What I'd like to know is where he came from. If you really looked at that swamp there was no way a monster that size could fit in it."

"Who cares?" Derek said with his mouth full. "It was just a movie."

Cam took a huge bite of pizza. "Yeah, I know, but if I'd made that movie, I would've made it more realistic. A monster that big has to come from someplace where there's space to fit it. And look at those giant cockroaches. They —"

"Cockroaches!" Wendy shuddered again.

"I know the perfect birthday present for Wendy," Alan said slyly.

"No!" Wendy shrieked, turning to me. "Stop him, Lori!"

"I think the girl should've fallen in love with the monster instead," I said. "He was nicer than the men — nobody understood him, that's all."

"Gross!" Debi made a disgusted face. "All that slime!"

"So she likes monsters better than men," Derek said in a voice that was barely audible.

My jaw dropped. A sour feeling twisted my stomach. Under the table someone gave my foot a reassuring nudge.

Wendy came to my defence. "Well, you've got to admit she's got a point. Those guys were pretty dumb."

"They didn't even try to communicate with it," I persisted. "All they wanted to do was kill it."

"All that green blood!" Alan clapped his hand to his chest as if he'd been shot.

"You guys!" Wendy sputtered. "How'm I supposed to enjoy my pizza?"

"With great pleasure," Derek said smugly. "After all, I paid."

I slumped. It wasn't working. I just didn't feel like part of the group. They were still nice kids and they cared about me. But I wasn't on the same wave-length anymore. I wasn't even sure I liked myself very much. I stared across the room at the brightly lit video games. "Still working at McDonald's, Wendy?" I asked.

"Sure am," she replied cheerfully. "Monday, Wednesday, Friday, four to seven. How come you guys never come see me?"

Derek snickered. "How's the babysitting business? Come on, Wright, admit it — you really get off on stinky diapers and snotty noses?"

My face flamed. "Those kids are people just like you, Derek Mahler. Anyway, you used to wear diapers too."

Everybody cracked up.

"No, I never!" Derek protested, covering his face.

"Born potty-trained, eh?" Alan thumped the table. "The world's one and only!"

Cam shot me an odd look. For an instant I stared back, wondering what he was thinking. But I didn't dare let myself wonder too much. Half the time guys seemed worthless, and who wanted to get hurt again anyway?

I got up and wandered over to the video games. For some reason I was shaking. Seizing the wheel of the racing car game, I plugged in a quarter.

"Look out!" Alan yelled. "Lady driver!"

I turned and gave him a plastic smile. "I know how to drive." And then I put all my attention to the game, swerving to avoid the road hazards that kept popping up in front of me. My jaw clenched. Sweat moistened my palms as my car crashed and burst into flames, only to magically reappear on the road. I kept on driving until *Game over* flashed on the screen in front of me.

What on earth was I doing standing there with a dumb video game feeling sorry for myself and mad at my friends? Even Cam was talking about dumb things like monsters. Why wasn't he different now? After all, his grandfather had died. Maybe it was worse being stuck with a bratty brother who was the centre of attention, who got away with murder because he was sick. I spun the wheel, even though it no longer controlled the image on the screen. The car spun off the road again and burst into flames. Once more *Game over* flashed in red letters.

Tears welled in my eyes and an aching knot formed in my throat. I clung harder to the wheel and squeezed my eyes shut.

"Game's over, Lori." Cam had come over and was standing beside me.

"Is it ever," I said through clenched teeth.

The juke box exploded with a loud country and western twang. "Is it the kid?" he asked.

I looked up at him. There wasn't a chance anybody at the table could hear us over the music. "He's bratty as usual," I muttered. There was no way I could even begin to describe the scene that had sent Heather away.

Cam spun the wheel, pretending to play just as I had done. "What's wrong then? These days you've got the sense of humour of a run-over skunk."

"Thanks a lot!" I choked. And then the tears really spilled.

"Hey, you maniac drivers!" Alan yelled.

"We're heading over to Wendy's. Can you tear yourselves away from the game?"

I grabbed the steering wheel and tensed every muscle in my body.

"The lady needs some driving lessons," Cam said lazily. "We'll be over after I teach her how to keep from wiping out every time."

Alan guffawed.

"They're gone," he said a moment later.

I wiped my eyes fiercely and sat down at an empty table. Cam sat silently across from me, his dark eyes asking questions. I looked away. "Things aren't so great at home right now," I mumbled.

"Derek always said you took things like a trooper," he said slowly. "Your kid brother gets cancer, you take it like a trooper. Your boyfriend dumps you, you take it like —"

I raised my head. "Is that what he said? That he dumped *me?*"

Cam drummed his fingers on the table. "Didn't he?"

"No! *I* called it off."

Cam's eyes widened. Then he began to laugh. "That Mahler," he said, shaking his head. "I should've known."

"What else did he say?" I demanded furiously. "What other lies has he been telling about me?" A cast-off napkin shredded into pieces in my hands.

Cam reached across the table and took the wad from me. "Does it matter? Everybody knows

Derek's just Derek. Look, Lori, if it bothers you so much, how come you keep rubbing your face in it?"

"It's not Derek anymore." My voice broke but I made myself keep talking, even though one reason for my misery was right in front of me. "I'm just not in the same space as everybody else and it doesn't work if I try to pretend."

"I know where you're coming from," Cam tapped his fingers once more. The hospital visit together leaped into my mind and I looked away. "It's probably harder for you," he went on in a low voice. "Granddad was an old man. He had a good life. And I know he's at peace now. Jamie's only a kid." His fingers knotted together and strained backwards.

It dawned on me as I stared at his large hands. He wasn't smoking. He looked nervous as anything but he wasn't smoking. He hadn't smoked all evening. In fact, I couldn't remember when I'd last seen him with a cigarette. "Did you quit?" I blurted out. "Smoking I mean?"

He looked away. "Yeah."

A new ache settled in my throat. "That's great." And then I was crying again.

In a quick motion he was sitting on the bench beside me. A moment later his arm came around me. "Okay, trooper, what else is wrong?"

Surprise tingled through me. Then I sagged against him.

He squeezed my shoulder. "Come on, you can tell your old buddy Cam. I get the feeling I could say the sky's blue and you'd cry about that too."

A strangled giggle choked out of me and I nodded against his chest.

"It's okay," he said softly. "Hey, would you rather cry in the truck? No point in flooding the pizza parlour."

I nodded again and let him get our jackets. In the still coldness outside, the tears made shivery streaks across my cheeks. I shuddered. His arm settled around my shoulder once more.

The pickup was freezing. I cried and hung onto him. "Nothing fits anymore," I said when I could talk again. "It all used to fit together — friends, school, family. Now nothing matches up and I just feel — lost."

He sighed and pulled me into his lap.

A nervous giggle popped out of me. "You make me feel like I'm three years old!"

"So what's the difference sometimes?" he said darkly. "Especially if you're hurting inside."

A new onslaught of tears spilled, but then I relaxed. He understood. He really did. He wasn't making me pretend nothing was wrong, the way Derek so often had. I sat there resting in the comfort he was offering. It seemed ages since someone had been so all-there for me.

He shifted his position, hitting the horn. We both jumped. But even though he'd jerked away, the horn kept right on blaring.

"Damn!" he muttered. "Stupid truck's falling apart." He opened the door.

"What's wrong with the horn?" Suddenly I was balancing precariously between tears and giggles.

140

"Wiring." He got out and lifted the hood.

The awful noise continued. At last it got the best of me. Here we were in a half-full parking lot, horn blasting non-stop. Probably everybody for blocks around was wondering what was going on.

A few minutes later Cam was back, shaking his head. "I can't figure it out. Guess I'll just have to drive it like this."

The smothered giggles exploded out of me.

In the half-light of the parking lot Cam turned to me with a self-mocking grin. "You've got to admit it could've been worse. We could've been — oh, God, forget it!" Embarrassed, he turned away and jammed the key into the ignition.

Right away I was silenced, remembering the time he'd kissed me at the lake. Was he thinking about it too? For an instant the unspoken question dangled electrically between us. I pulled back slightly, my heart thudding in my ears. And all around us the din of the horn continued.

The motor whined and protested, not wanting to start. Abruptly Cam was distant, concentrating on the truck.

"I'll scrape the windows," I said, subdued. I found the scraper and went to work on the inside. If the others saw us now they'd really dish it out. Put a guy and a girl in a vehicle with windows frozen over both inside and out and usually they'd been doing something more entertaining than crying. Furtively I glanced at Cam as he pleaded with the reluctant engine. Did he feel that way about me or was he just being nice? Maybe the whole thing at the lake had been for show, just like with everyone else.

The engine turned over. Cam gave a sigh of relief. "Here, I'll get the outside," he said gruffly, reaching for the scraper. "Keep your foot on the gas, will you? And whatever you do, don't let the engine die."

I watched the frost crystals compact and then fall away as broad streaks of clear glass appeared before me. And the horn kept right on blaring.

"Want to go to Wendy's?" he asked as he got back in.

I shook my head, afraid to look at him. "I think I just want to go home."

"Sure." His foot settled firmly on the accelerator. I scooted out of the driver's seat. Lurching like a lame horse, the truck pulled out into the street.

It was too soon when he stopped in front of our house, the horn noisy as ever. "I'm afraid to let this thing quit," he said. And again there was the self-mocking grin.

"Cam, thanks. For everything." How else could I say it without sounding all dumb and mushy? Or without making it seem as if it meant nothing? I looked up at him, wishing I could read some answers in his face.

With a breezy wave he dismissed me. "Sure, anytime. Take it easy, lady."

"Take care." It wasn't much more than a whisper, so I couldn't tell whether or not he heard as I shut the door.

142

# 13
# Friday the 13th

The daycare Valentine's Day party was held on Friday the thirteenth. It was the same day the schools shut down for teachers' conventions, the same day as one of Jamie's chemotherapy appointments at the hospital.

I awoke to the sound of the wind howling past the corners of the house. When I looked out the window a cloud of blowing snow made it difficult to see even to the end of the block. I was tempted to burrow back under the covers but the smell of frying bacon tugged at me. If Dad was going to the effort of making a nice breakfast with Mom already gone for the day, there was no way I could stay in bed.

Jamie sat glumly at the table with only a glass of milk in front of him.

"So it's that time again." Dad looked as if he felt guilty with his plate of bacon, eggs and hash browns.

"I don't want any more chemotherapy," Jamie said dully.

"I'll be back in time to take you to the hospital," Dad said. "Ten-thirty, right?"

Jamie scowled. "Ten-thirty next year."

I couldn't help feeling sorry for him as I sat there sipping my orange juice. His arms already bore enough needle scars to make him look like a drug addict. "Only two more months of chemo after this," I said.

"Just shut up, okay?" Jamie cried. His face reddened and then, to my surprise, tears streaked down his cheeks. He got up quickly. "Don't *I* ever get any say in things? I've *had* it! I just can't take any more!" He charged up the stairs and his bedroom door slammed, followed by a series of crashes and dull thuds which jarred the ceiling directly overhead.

I looked at Dad, aghast. He was stroking his beard and his eyes were moist. We sat there a few minutes without speaking. The house shuddered with each impact of Jamie's fury.

"Sounds like he's wrecking his room," I said weakly.

At that same instant Dad got up. Without replying, he went upstairs.

I sat there staring at the breakfast table. The cold egg on my plate was beginning to congeal. A half-eaten strip of bacon was speared on Dad's fork. In a way I felt like that piece of bacon — up in the air, forgotten. But quickly I shook myself. Jamie had it far tougher than I did. At least I could still escape to school and forget about everything for a while. I could still get together with my friends and pretend nothing had changed. The cancer was in my brother's body, not mine, and it was Jamie's body and Jamie's emotions that took the brunt of the disease and its harsh treatment. When it came right down to it, he had every reason to go a little berserk every once in a while.

I got up and slowly began clearing the table. I'd lost track of how many times things had worked out this way — left by myself in the kitchen because of a crisis involving Jamie. But when I really thought about it, I knew that things could've turned out far worse.

I washed the dishes and then dumped the contents of a manila envelope onto the table. Bright valentines scattered across the dark surface, perky reds and pinks almost seeming to laugh in defiance at the blizzard outside. Methodically I began writing names on each card. Melissa who loved to be swung around as if she were flying. Solemn, curly-haired Eric who so often stood there with his thumb in his mouth. Tiny Jonathan whose face was always smudged and smiling. Scott.

I paused. At times our impish red-headed problem was my favourite child of all, while at other moments I wished I could lock him in the supplies cabinet. He was a complex little boy compared to many of the others, one minute getting into the most unlikely scrapes and making a person want to scream in frustration, and the next instant looking up with such a trusting gaze that even the most hardened criminal would melt a little inside. During the past week Scott had been more hyperactive than ever and very difficult to control. Just the day before he'd really given me a scare when I found him under the table with the record player plug in his mouth. A cold trickle of fear skittered between my ribs as I thought how easily something could happen to that little boy.

Dad came back downstairs, interrupting my thoughts. "I'll be back in a couple of hours, Lori," he said as he bundled up in his down jacket and his boots.

I didn't ask how Jamie was. The house was quiet, so the worst must be over.

I sighed and went back to signing the cards. There didn't seem to be much else to do. For some reason I saved Cam's card until last. *Love, Lori.* The pen seemed to move of its own accord. I stared. That was exactly the way I'd signed all the other cards, but I didn't dare do it with Cam's.

His dark-eyed, dark-haired image flashed before me. Cam had become very much a part of my life during the past months, yet in a maddening way he remained elusive. My shy new feelings for him made me wonder if I was being ridiculous, but the memory of those few times of intense sharing had a way of slicing right through all the turmoil and showing me something startlingly new and clear.

The telephone rang.

It was Dad. "Lori?" His voice was tense. "I'm

going to have to ask you a big favour. There's been a problem with the car and I won't be able to take Jamie to the hospital."

A put-upon feeling began swelling inside me and I wrapped my fingers in the coiled cord. "What do you want me to do?"

Dad sighed. "I'm on campus. I've tried calling a cab but all the companies say with this blizzard it might be four hours before I get a taxi."

There was something he wasn't telling me. "What happened?"

"I slid into a delivery van on the way here and smashed the fender," Dad said wearily. "Don't worry, I'm not hurt. But at the moment the car is useless. I need you to drive Jamie to the hospital."

"Dad!" I looked around the house, so quiet I might as well be home alone. If I knew my brother he'd never co-operate. Without Mom or Dad around it would take a crane or a bulldozer to get him to the hospital.

"Mom's car is still home," Dad continued. "I drove her to her meeting because she was worried about parking downtown all day in this storm. Can you do this for me? Traffic's moving very slowly. You'll just have to watch out for other drivers in trouble and make sure you don't get stuck in a drift."

"Well, I —" Weakly I cupped the receiver in both hands. "Why don't I pick you up and you take Jamie."

"Please, Lori, I'm way over on the other side

of town. Drifts are bad out here. It would be much safer for you to do what I ask."

"What if I crash Mom's car?" I demanded.

Dad sounded impatient. "I don't expect you will. The hospital isn't far and the streets in our part of town are relatively clear."

"Well — yeah, I guess so," I said dubiously.

"Thanks, Lori." Dad sounded relieved. "I knew I could count on you." He hung up.

Flustered, I looked out into the raging blizzard. Mom's car was a snow-covered mound sitting in the street. Just getting the snow off the windows looked like a major undertaking, and warming it up — not to mention getting Jamie *into* it. I took a long breath and went upstairs.

There was no answer when I knocked on Jamie's door, so I walked in. I choked back a gasp of anger and dismay. His room looked like a junk heap. The floor was covered with a tangle of clothes, upside-down drawers, books, tools and pieces of gadgets. The mirror was smashed. His desk was tipped over and his chair lay on its back with one leg missing. Jamie was lying on his bed facing the wall. Little bits of foam were scattered in a trail between his pillow and the floor.

"Jamie?" I said shakily.

He didn't move.

"Jamie."

He still didn't respond, so I went over and shook him. "Jamie!"

In a tight, bitter voice he began swearing at me.

148

I didn't know what to do. One look around the room had shown me the enormity of my brother's feelings. With another deep breath I said, "Jamie, I'm supposed to take you to the hospital. Dad had a wreck. He's okay but he can't get here in time."

At last my brother turned to face me. His eyes were puffy and red from crying. "I'm not going and you can't make me. Mom and Dad can't either. Nobody —"

"Jamie, you *have* to! How can they cure you if —"

"Nobody can make me! It's my life and I'm deciding."

"That's right, Jamie" — I bent to pick up a chunk of the mirror and tossed it in the tipped-over wastebasket — "it's your *life*. You know what happens if cancer —"

"Yes, I know what happens. It's *my* decision."

"You're just a kid. Mom and Dad —"

Jamie sat up, his eyes blazing. "They can't make me! I'll leave home!"

The thought of Jamie battling a Saskatchewan winter on his own, sick with Hodgkin's disease and easy to identify with his bald head, tugged at my heart. Suddenly I was swallowing hard. "You can't do that. Where would you go?"

"Why would I tell you? Just get out of here, okay? I want to be alone."

"Jamie, please. I — I care about you and I want you to get better." I gave up trying to hold back the tears. All of us in the family were caught in the clutches of the disease and it was silly to try to pretend we weren't. "Jamie, I really mean that. I want you to get better and the odds —"

"Odds? What are odds anyway with something like cancer? Either you get better or you don't." He spoke as if he'd thought it through thousands of times, as if it were so boring he didn't even want to be bothered.

"You make it sound like you don't want to get better," I said. "Like you really don't care."

"I care." His voice was flippant. "But I've had it with the chemo, so that's that."

I was tempted to call Dad, but what could he do from the university? I wouldn't even be able to get Jamie to the phone to talk to him. I set the wastebasket upright and flung in more chunks of mirror. They broke into even smaller fragments. "You don't care. You just want to throw it all away. Your whole life. You're usually a smart kid but this is the dumbest thing I've heard in a long time. Well, you just wait. In ten years I'll tell people about this really smart brother I used to have — how he probably would've been a scientist, only he threw it all away because he didn't want to take his medicine."

Jamie stood up fast and punched me in the arm, so hard that a heavy bruised feeling throbbed in my muscles. "You get out of my room!" he yelled. "Or I'll hit you again, harder."

I went downstairs and sagged onto the chesterfield. It was hard to remember a time when I'd felt so defeated and alone. Jamie was acting as if he didn't care about anything, even after I told him how much I cared. This time I couldn't call Heather or go find Mom. Somehow I would have to get Jamie to the hospital — or else give up and get Mom or Dad to reschedule his chemotherapy. Maybe that wouldn't be so awful. Dad really was asking a lot.

At some point I became aware of the whine of stuck tires spinning in snow. The sound went on and on, so finally I bundled up to go help. The raging wind buffeted me, blasting snow into my face and forcing me backwards. It was like trying to walk into a wall, a wall that was sometimes there and sometimes not, leaving me staggering nearly out of control. When I reached the car I was glad I had come. Old Mrs. Beattie was sitting behind the wheel and another elderly woman was trying to push. When I added my efforts the car rocked forward bit by bit and finally eased itself out of the snowy rut.

At least *one* thing had gone right. And then the obvious solution flashed through my mind. I walked up the Duncans' front steps and rang the bell.

"That little twerp!" John said when I'd explained. "I'll see what I can do."

I led the way into the house. "Jamie!" I yelled. "John's here."

There was no answer.

"What's the matter, J.C.?" John called. "Can't take a little medicine, eh?" He went up the stairs with purposeful strides. "Hey, J.C.? You still there?"

I went to a window and watched the snow whipping past. My arm still hurt.

"*Medicine?*" Finally Jamie's voice sounded on the stairs. "That stuff's poison! The mechlorethamine's related to the mustard gas they used in World War I. That's what makes me throw up and knocks back my white count. The procarbazine knocks back my white count some more. Think I like having no white blood count and getting sick? Think I *like* the way the vincristine keeps me bald at the ripe old age of twelve? The pred—"

John grabbed Jamie's shoulders and shook him. "What are a few chemicals?" he screamed back.

Jamie looked stunned, then resigned. "Yeah, I guess so," he muttered. He looked at me. "Sorry I hit you, Lor."

"It's okay," I mumbled. "I'm going to warm up the car."

There was such a heavy load of snow on the windshield that the plastic scraper broke. The wind was an awesome force behind me, plastering the windows with fresh snow almost as quickly as I brushed it off with broad strokes of my arm. Finally Jamie and John came out to help.

It took all my concentration to keep the car moving through the deep snow. Everywhere I looked drivers were fish-tailing and getting stuck. Without warning a car nearby slid through a stop sign and headed straight toward us. I jammed my hand on the horn.

The car stalled. But there was no crash. Jamie began yelling out the window.

"Let's park and catch a bus," I said, shaken.

"Are you kidding?" Jamie cried. "Want me to throw up all over the bus? In front of all those strangers?"

"You're not going to —"

"Oh, yes, I am. Every time. That's why Mom always brings —" He turned on me. "I bet you forgot it."

I sighed. "Jamie, I'm not a mind reader. Forgot what?"

Horns were honking behind us.

"We're blocking traffic," John remarked.

Embarrassed, I started the car and pulled over to the side. Wet snow splattered onto the windshield, erasing the rest of the world. "Forgot what? How'm I supposed to know? I've never done this before, remember?"

"The basin, buffalo brain. What am I gonna throw up in?"

"Why didn't *you* remember? It's your problem. Now I —"

"Cut it out, you guys," John said. "Let's just get there. Hospitals have that kind of thing, you know."

"You'd make me throw up in the street like an old wino," Jamie muttered.

I had plenty of replies about bratty brothers.

But I started the car instead and headed toward the hospital at a steady crawl.

John went in with Jamie and I waited and waited in the waiting room. It was full of patients and their families. Many looked weary and drawn. A little girl with wispy hair sat very quietly next to her mother. Nearby was an elderly woman whose complexion was jaundiced, wearing a hat with turquoise feathers. No hair peeked out from underneath. In another chair sat a sturdy looking man who was probably a farmer — with blue lines drawn across one side of his neck. It was a place of pain and fear and desperate hope and I could understand why Jamie hated to come.

At last he and John rounded a corner. Jamie was a changed person. Washed out and off-colour already, he stumbled toward the exit carrying a plastic kidney basin. "C'mon, let's get outta here."

John fell in step beside me. "Good news!"

In a place like this it was impossible to think anyone might have good news. "What?"

John smiled through his thick lenses. "His chest X-ray is clear! No tumor left!"

I caught up with Jamie. "That's fantastic! Does —"

"Shut up and get me home. Fast."

Hurt, I stomped ahead to brush the fresh snow off the windshield. Without a word, Jamie lay down on the back seat.

Nervously I started the car. John got in beside me.

154

"God, I feel awful," Jamie moaned. "I wish I was home already. You'll probably get us stuck and —"

"Cut it out!" I jerked the car into reverse. "You don't need to treat me like a —"

"Watch out for the Cadillac," John said.

The vomiting began before we made it home. The sounds and the smell turned my stomach. I clenched the steering wheel tighter. Little drops of perspiration beaded my temples.

In the back seat Jamie sighed and swore.

"That's great about your X-rays." My voice came out tight and somehow false and I bit my lip. It *was* great. It was fantastic. But mixed up with the relief was a lot of hurt and bewilderment.

John helped me get Jamie into the house, then upstairs to his room. "You did some pretty decent driving in that storm," he said, catching me by surprise.

"Thanks," I said, touched.

Jamie lay there grimly. "She did okay," he agreed. "We didn't crash and we didn't get stuck."

I didn't know what to say. Several hours remained before I needed to be at the daycare for the Valentine's party. There wasn't much for me to do, so self-consciously I began picking up books from the floor.

John looked around the chaotic room. "You really did it this time, J.C. What's your mom gonna think?"

"That I ought to be chained to my bed and —"

But Jamie broke off and retreated into a familiar ominous silence. A moment later he was sick again.

After the whole exhausting ordeal I wasn't so sure I wanted to go to a Valentine's Day party for preschoolers. On the other hand, Cam would be there. *Maybe* something would happen.

# 14
# Shock!

The daycare centre almost felt more like home than our house did. It was noisy. I belonged. There were too many things to be done, things like tying party hats beneath small chins, and punching valentine cookie cutters into peanut butter sandwiches and setting the results on plates. When I got a free moment I slipped my valentine cards into the shoe boxes the children had decorated. But when I got to Cam's box I hesitated.

"Lori?" Jan was calling me. "Could you go help with the singing? Oh, by the way, keep a close eye on Scott. He's having one of his days."

I groaned. A bad day for Scott usually meant a bad day for everyone.

Automatically my hand released Cam's valentine. I watched it slide through the slot. It was too late. I could hardly rummage through the box to pull it back out.

The children were already singing when I slipped into the room. Although I tiptoed in, instant commotion arose when both Scott and Kristi insisted on sitting in my lap. I scooped them up, settling one on each knee. Kristi leaned back against me, a warm contented little person. But Scott was a wiry bundle of energy. I stroked his curly red hair, hoping it would help him stop squirming.

Cam grinned at me, released a few resounding chords from his guitar and began *Old MacDonald*. He sang with a pleasant baritone voice and made such wonderful animal sounds that shivers ran up my spine. There was a kind of glow in his face and he was so in tune with the children it seemed as if a spell had been cast over most of them. Eric was sitting up straight and singing, not slouching with his thumb in his mouth. Amy's pert face was bright with enthusiasm. Melissa was swaying as she sang. But in my lap Scott was reaching for Kristi's shoelaces and then, in the next instant, playing with his party hat.

"You were fantastic!" I told Cam afterwards. "You should go on TV!"

He shrugged. "It's fun. I'm kinda thinking about being a teacher someday."

Then I remembered the good news about Jamie. "Guess what! Jamie's X-rays are clear," I said, needing to share it.

Cam drew back slightly with a surprised smile. "All right!" And he pulled me into a one-armed hug. For an instant everything seemed to stop. All I was aware of was Cam and how close we were.

But the daycare was continuing on in its normal manner. Ryan was running around shrieking. Andrea had started blowing at the paper doilies on people's party hats and not everyone liked it. Scott was creeping toward the unsupervised refreshment table.

"Scott!" I said sharply. He looked up with a guilty look in his blue eyes, one small hand poised directly above the cake.

Just as suddenly Cam was headed in another direction. "Christopher, please don't pop the balloons."

I didn't get another chance to talk to him until after it happened.

Jan and I were in the kitchen washing dishes with Kristi's help. Jan was reassuring Kristi that her father would never forget something as important as a valentine for his little girl.

Out of the corner of my eye I thought I saw a ball of white light, thought I heard a faint popping sound. It was gone so quickly that when I turned to look nothing seemed changed. I shook my head, deciding I must be imagining things.

But then the confusion began. Voices babbled in the playroom, not the ordinary din of children having a good time. *"Scott!"* someone cried out. One of the staff raced past. I heard the dial rotating on the office phone. Jan and I exchanged startled glances. We ran out to see what was wrong.

The lights were off. The children were milling around, out of control. Cam was kneeling on the floor, bending over the prone figure of a child. It was Scott.

"What —"

"Electric shock." One of the morning staff answered my question. Tears were running down her face. Her voice was jittery. "I don't know how he managed it — key in an electric outlet."

I began trembling. Nausea kneaded my stomach. My face went sweaty. Cam was giving artificial respiration.

"Lori?" Jan was shaking my shoulder. "Are you okay? We have to see about the kids."

I was numb for the last bit of the afternoon. Scott . . . electric shock . . . Cam . . . artificial respiration. Thought fragments tumbled senselessly through my mind. Would Scott be all right? Where was Cam so I could ask him? Scott . . . hospitals could accomplish some amazing things. Maybe he'd be okay. Where *was* Cam? The telephone was ringing in the office. But it was near closing time and nobody seemed to need me. Most of the children had already gone home, some of them still unaware of what had happened. I wouldn't be able to do any good anyway.

The howling storm engulfed me. It was getting dark. I wrapped my scarf around my face and ducked into the icy wind. It was hard to make out the bus stop through the white sheets of blowing snow. Scott, that sweet little boy — Suddenly the wind was driving me back toward the dark hulk of the building. When someone seized my arm, a squawk sounded in my throat. I tried to jerk away.

"Lori, it's only me, Cam."

I looked up at him. "Where were you? I mean, after —"

"Nadine called from the hospital. They revived him."

My throat filled with tears. Suddenly I was shuddering violently. Cam's arm came around me, pulling me tightly against him.

"I'll take you home," he said.

There was nothing I could say. Cam was like my own private shelter against the storm, against the cold, against the terrifying event. I wanted to tell him that he had probably saved Scott's life with the artificial respiration, that I thought he was wonderful. But he kept holding me and the words stayed inside.

His pickup didn't want to start. The starter whined lazily and the engine made several half-hearted attempts before it finally coughed to life. I sat there, numb, huddled against Cam, blinking each time the windshield wipers passed before my face.

"He's going to be all right," Cam said in a dazed voice. "God, I was so scared."

I thought of Cam's grandfather. Cam had already seen death, face to face. He'd probably been even more frightened than I was. I thought of John and his close call. I thought of Jamie, who seemed to be getting better. It was like a collection of mismatched puzzle pieces trying to fit together into one picture. But they wouldn't fit and I was still shaking.

Three blocks from our house a shuddering metallic clanking pierced through the engine. The truck stopped. Cam moaned and coaxed but it wouldn't start again. Finally he pounded on the wheel and got out. I followed silently.

For every step of the way the wind flung snow in our faces. It caught in our eyelashes and tried to clog our nostrils. I walked along rapidly beside Cam. "Mom or Dad will take you home," I said.

He glanced at me with pain in his face. "I think it's the end of the road for that truck," he mumbled.

I had the feeling he was talking about a lot more than his truck. "It can't be fixed?"

He shook his head. "It'd cost a fortune — if anyone could do it."

"It's really great, what you did with Scott," I said hesitantly.

He shrugged. "I was closest. I just can't help wondering — if I'd been watching him better . . ."

I touched his arm. "Scott could've done the same thing with three people watching him. Besides, you said he's going to be okay."

"I know." He didn't sound very sure of himself.

"Hello?" Mom's cheerful call sounded the minute I opened the front door.

Behind me Cam kicked off his boots. Then he walked across the living room and slumped on the chesterfield.

"Hello?" Mom peered out of the kitchen.

I went to meet her. "We had a scary time at the daycare. Scott just about got electrocuted and Cam gave him artificial respiration."

"Oh, my goodness!" Mom's concern was mirrored in her eyes. "Is he all right?"

"What happened?" Jamie yelled from upstairs.

I didn't want to repeat the news. I went back to sit with Cam. His face was closed, no longer revealing his pain. Sir Thomas Catt had emerged from his hiding place under the chesterfield and was sniffing at Cam's jacket.

Cam's large hand slid down the cat's back and Sir Thomas arched, then relaxed with a loud rumbling purr.

"Looks like you've got a friend for life." My hands felt absurdly empty as Cam patted my cat. Scott would still be in the hospital and no doubt his already overworked mother would be at his bedside, worried to tears. My mind told me that the whole incident had been one of those horrible accidents that just happen, that really Scott was very lucky — but my emotions didn't want to accept it. It was *Scott,* not some strange child in a newspaper headline. If Cam hadn't thought quickly someone else probably would have. But it had been Cam and now he was obviously feeling the effects.

"Hey, kitty," he muttered, "do you really have nine lives?"

Jamie burst into the living room, his bald head gleaming in the lamplight. "*What* happened?"

Irritation snapped through me. If Jamie threw a scene now — "I thought you were sick."

"The old MOPP didn't hit so hard this time. What's going on?" He stood there in his pyjamas, grimacing at me.

I sighed. "A kid at the daycare just about got electrocuted."

"Oh." Jamie sat down in the reclining chair, his bare foot tapping against the footrest. "Did he sizzle?"

"Jamie!"

"It wasn't very pretty." Cam's large frame remained tense as he stroked the cat.

I shot Jamie a warning look and stood up. "Want some hot chocolate, Cam?"

"Yeah, sure," he said listlessly.

When I returned with a steaming mug, Cam was still petting Sir Thomas. Jamie lay sprawled on the floor poking at the computer keyboard. I handed Cam the hot chocolate and then stood there feeling useless.

*ZAP!* The word leaped out at me from the TV screen.

"Cut it out, Jamie," I muttered.

There was an indescribable expression on Jamie's face. Suddenly I knew he wasn't just being obnoxious. That computer might be another way of expressing his feelings — in a way far more constructive than the treatment he'd given his bedroom.

"Key in a plug-in," Jamie mused. "Was he in water or something, or touching a heater vent?"

"I don't know," Cam said wearily. "Nobody was watching."

A sudden impulse seized me, sending my heart racing. Moving slowly, as if I did this kind of thing every day, I went behind Cam and started rubbing his taut shoulders.

For an instant he tensed. Then he sighed and leaned farther back into the cushions.

It was Jamie who broke the silence. "I wonder if that kid had an experience like John's."

I looked up, startled. "An after-death experience? Maybe he did. I wonder —"

Without warning, Cam was rigid.

"Scary," Jamie went on. "But John said it made him quit being afraid of it anymore."

His words were like a charge of static in the quiet room. It was odd hearing my brother speak so candidly. Perhaps venting his rage on his bedroom had changed something inside him. He was actually acting human. And it was clear that he was still afraid of what the future might bring.

"I think you're okay once it happens." Cam's words were low and intense. "I know my grandfather's at peace. I can feel it sometimes." His voice caught and his shoulders sagged.

A huge lump filled my throat. I wanted to throw my arms around him and hug him the way he'd held me. But he lurched to his feet and headed for the door.

"Cam!" His name wrenched out of me.

Without looking back he put on his boots. Cold air and snow swirled into the house for a moment and then he was gone.

My chin was wobbling. With a swift motion Mom was beside me, holding me. It was wonderful to be able to rest my head against her shoulder. I hadn't realized she'd known how I felt about Cam — and about Scott — and about Jamie.

# 15
# Forecast: Spring?

I couldn't sleep that night. I shifted from one position to another until the covers were a tangled trap. I got up and tried writing a note to Heather, but after flinging several crumpled attempts in the wastebasket, I gave up. At three in the morning I went downstairs and fixed myself a cup of hot chocolate. Outside the blizzard was still raging.

When I came back upstairs a line of light was spilling out from under Jamie's bedroom door. Suddenly I needed company. I knocked.

"Yeah?" he called out in a harsh whisper.

Hesitantly I went in. The room had been straightened up as much as possible, but the smashed mirror and broken chair were glaring reminders of Jamie's outburst. My brother was propped up against his pillow reading a book on computers.

"Whad'ya want?" he asked gruffly.

Gingerly I sat on his bed, looking away from the basin on his desk. "I can't sleep," I muttered.

"Who says I wasn't about to conk out?" he said.

I sighed. "I just needed to talk."

Jamie guffawed. "You? Talk to me? What's the matter, get hard up for friends all of a sudden?"

I winced. My brother seemed to be rapidly returning to his normal bratty state. "Jamie, it's after three in the morning. What am I supposed to do, call Heather and get her parents mad at me?"

Jamie shot me a silly grin. "So now I get to be Heather."

"Forget it." I stood up. "You'd never understand."

"About what?" Suddenly his voice was challenging.

I looked at him without speaking.

Jamie shook his head. "You know, a year ago it seemed like it always happened to the other guy, somebody you'd never even heard of. But then I got sick and — well, the world seems pretty different now."

He understood all right. I sat back down.

"No kidding," I muttered. A piece from one of Jamie's gadgets was on the floor, sticking out from under his bed. I bent over and picked it up. "It's hit Cam too," I added. "I wish —"

But Jamie was reaching for the basin.

I held my breath and tried not to gag as he vomited. "Want me to empty it?" I asked gingerly.

Jamie whooped. "How about that! My high-and-mighty sister volunteers to clean up my puke!"

I cringed. "Well, you're feeling rotten . . ."

"Nah, I'll do it. You'd probably throw up all the way to the bathroom." Jamie padded out into the hall. During his absence Sir Thomas leaped into my lap. It was reassuring to pet the warm, relaxed animal.

"You're kinda hung up on Cam, aren't you?" Jamie said as he crawled back into bed.

A hot, defensive feeling raced through me. "Maybe."

"He's not so bad," Jamie conceded.

I kicked the corner of the throw rug into a curled-over flap. "What a weird year."

"You said it," Jamie muttered. He tossed his book across the room. It skidded along a shelf, coming to rest against the wall.

"I bet it feels great to be okay again," I said cautiously.

For a moment he looked as if he were about to clam up. "The doc said no promises," he finally said. "But if I stay in remission long enough — say five years — they'll figure I'm cured."

My brother's face was so sombre I felt like hugging him, but I knew that would end the conversation in one clean sweep. "Kind of like having a clock ticking inside," I said.

"Or something." Jamie turned away from me. "Hey, look, I'm tired."

There was no missing the hint. "Thanks for talking," I said awkwardly.

By seven-thirty the wind had quieted and the clouds were gone. A heavy tiredness clamped over me, but even so I hadn't been able to sleep. I lay there a while longer. My bed was beginning to feel more like a trap than a place of rest. Did it seem that way to Jamie sometimes? Suddenly impatient, I got dressed and crept downstairs to put on my boots and jacket.

Outside, the air was clean and sweet with the smell of new snow. The sky was beginning to lighten in the east. The front steps were vague, shapeless mounds under the deep layer of snow, so I grabbed the snow shovel. The steady rhythm and firm scraping sound helped pull my head together. Scott was going to be all right. And Cam? My throat ached. What he'd been through was even more intense than my own experiences. And there was something between us waiting to emerge. Even Jamie had seen that.

I straightened up, stretched my back and went to work clearing off the sidewalk. Once I looked up the street in the direction of Cam's truck, but even the vehicles nearby were hard to recognize under their blanket of snow. As I put away the snow shovel I brushed against a spruce branch. White crystals dumped all over me.

I found myself wandering down toward the creek. The footbridge was spectacular with its coating of new snow. I looked at the smooth unbroken white, wishing I could soar over so as not to mar it. Finally I went across, carefully spacing my steps and trying not to kick the snow so I wouldn't leave a jumbled trail behind me.

I stepped up to the willow and ran my mitts along the grey crinkled bark. Sticking out of the snow-covered ice below was the grocery cart with my ski jutting out. I slid down onto the creek and yanked at the piece of ski, but of course it wouldn't move. With my tugging, the layer of snow was shed and the brightly coloured wood made a sharp contrast against the white all around.

Cam. I couldn't get him out of my mind. I clambered partway up the creek bank and in large letters began writing his name in the snow. Moving methodically, I tried to make each letter perfect.

Someone grabbed me. "Caught you in the act!"

I shrieked and rolled down the steep incline. He came rolling down with me, laughter sparkling in his dark eyes.

I fell into a sitting position and sat there, dazed and suddenly nervous. Cam pulled himself over to sit beside me. I couldn't help noticing how tired he looked and the stubble that blackened his chin. Then a huge dog muzzle was thrust into my face.

"Duke!" Cam snapped. "Back!" After a long silent moment he added, "That wasn't a joke, was it? I'm not just a charity case to feel sorry for?"

"What? A charity case?" I was shocked that he could even think it. All was quiet, except for the sound of Duke's breathing. Slowly I shook my head. "No. I never thought of you that way."

Cam gave a deep sigh and put his arm around me.

I sat absolutely still, despite the quivering anticipation darting through me. But Cam didn't move either. Suddenly impatient, I twisted upwards and kissed his bristly cheek.

He trembled slightly. "Oh, Lori." He spoke so softly I could hardly hear him. And then he kissed me.

It was as if he were asking me an important question with the gentle touch of his lips. The intensity of that question was almost frightening. Yet as I kissed him back I gave the answer as honestly as I could.

Something let go inside and a melting warmth swooned through me. It was unlike anything I'd experienced before, even with Derek. *I love you*, I thought dizzily.

A frenzied barking startled us. There was Duke, front paws braced, barking at us.

"Duke! Quiet!" Cam said sharply. Then he began to laugh. "He's never seen me do this before."

I leaned against him, slipping my arm around him. "He looks jealous!"

"He is." Cam glared at his dog, then kissed me again. His stomach let loose with an ominous growl.

I giggled. "Haven't you had breakfast yet?"

He grinned sheepishly. "Duke was so frisky this morning he wouldn't let me near the stove, and Mom's still asleep anyway."

For some reason I felt extraordinarily sure of myself. "Come on," I said, laughing. "I'll fix you something."

Cam reached for my hand as we clambered up the creek bank. We walked in silence for a few minutes. Then he spoke in a low voice. "I didn't mean to be rude and just take off like that last night. But — well, I've been missing Granddad an awful lot. He's still on my mind all the time. And then with what happened to Scott and my truck breaking down — I guess I was kinda coming unglued."

A soft warmth crept through me as I smiled up at him. This was the real Cam Wright, unmasked, trusting me — and someone I could trust. "It's okay," I said.

He sighed and swung my hand gently. Duke bounded ahead of us, scattering puffs of flying snow. Again we walked in silence.

Maybe Cam wasn't the only one who'd gone around wearing a mask. I certainly had, but I hadn't quite realized it until Jamie got sick. And what about Jamie? How could I even begin to understand the pain and fear he'd been through, all kept to himself? Respect and admiration for my kid brother surged through me. In Jamie's case the disease had been pushed back, maybe for good. That meant I still had a chance to get to know the person my brother really was. And if our exchanges last night and early this morning were any indication of who Jamie really was, he was worth getting to know better.

I couldn't hold back a bashful smile as I led Cam up the front steps. He had been over to our house so many times already but this time was different. It was a beginning. Or had last night been the beginning? I was too elated — and too tired — to try to figure it out just then.

It was Jamie, not Mom or Dad, who wandered into the kitchen at the sound of clattering pans. "What's for —" He pulled back. In the doorway to the laundry room a mournful Duke thumped his tail against the floor. Jamie rubbed his eyes. "Am I seeing things, or is this Incredible Hunk the second?"

"Jamie —"

Cam laughed. "Me or the dog?" He stuck out a hand to my brother. "I hear you've got a pretty good track record, kid. Good going."

Jamie's face was solemn as he shook Cam's hand. But then he stretched. "Can you guys cook enough for three people? I've been throwing up all night and I'm *starved*."

Cam grinned and wrapped an arm around me. "Better ask the cook."

I gave him a nudge in the ribs and smirked up at him. "So all you really want is food."

"Oh, yeah?" he retorted. "If that's what you think —"

Jamie was standing there, a skinny bald-headed figure in flannel pyjamas. "Who's cooking?"

I glanced at Cam. He grinned. We both looked at Jamie. "You are." I held out the package of bacon. Cam offered him the carton of eggs.

"No!" Jamie yelped. "I can't cook!"

"Sure you can," Cam said. "I hear you're a fast learner."

"It'll have to be a committee job," I said, giggling. "Jamie'd probably grease the pans with Mom's valve oil, and Cam, you wouldn't be able to find anything. I'll supervise."

Both of them turned on me. "*You* do it!"

"No!" I cowered, laughing.

The telephone rang.

"You guys cook," I called as I dashed to answer it. "I've got to get the phone."

It was Heather. "I hope I'm not calling too early," she said. "But I couldn't wait to hear about yesterday. Did anything happen?"

For an instant I drew a blank. She certainly wasn't asking about Jamie, and she wouldn't have heard about Scott. I shook myself. With everything that had happened the previous day, Heather was practically in a different time zone. And then I remembered. She'd been trying to convince me that Cam would give me something special in my valentine box at the daycare. With a start I realized I'd left it at the centre — and so had Cam. I drew in a shaky breath, trying to contain my excitement so it wouldn't spill over into the kitchen where Cam or Jamie could hear.

"I can't talk right now," I said in a hushed voice. "He's here."

"Right now?" she squealed. "It's not even nine in the morning! Oh, Lori, you've got to tell me all about it! I can hardly wait!"

"I'll call you back," I promised and hung up with a smile.

Back in the kitchen Cam was nursing the bacon as it sizzled in the skillet. Jamie was measuring out milk and dumping it into a saucepan. I leaned against the door frame. "Looks like you guys have everything under control."

"Oh, yeah?" Jamie retorted. "How'm I supposed to know how much stuff to put in?"

"Read the directions, silly."

Jamie began reading loudly, in French.

"Show-off!" I laughed.

"So what do I do now?" he demanded.

"You turn on the burner."

Muttering about child labour laws, my brother turned to the stove.

Cam looked at me with a warm smile in his dark eyes.

Everything felt wonderfully back to normal, only with a different focus. Jamie had more chemotherapy to endure and *then* he'd feel better and his hair would grow back. Cam was still coming to grips with the loss of his grandfather, but the way he was handling it was turning him into a very special person. I still had some raw spots inside, scars from the events of the long, cold winter. My parents must have some too. But we were all weathering it, and now I felt so much closer to everyone.

In a mysterious way the interlocking puzzle pieces were beginning to fit together. Part of the picture was Lori Carmichael — a changed Lori

Carmichael, yet still the same person who had felt free as the wind running along the creek dike only four months ago.

It was as if the brilliant searing light of the sundogs had been at work on all of us — Jamie, Cam, myself — burning away childish innocence in the cold hard light of reality. Of life.

But another season was coming. No matter what happened, spring would be around sooner or later, with its promise of new growth, of new life. I could feel it.

# Acknowledgements

It is impossible to adequately thank certain people — our families, our friends — whose loving support helped us through the many years of Michael's illness. Dana and Phil, Ken and Cheryl, there simply are no words that can express my gratitude for all that you gave during the final chapters. Kathy and Ken, you would have done the same if you had lived nearby; your concern was with us throughout. For John, our son, a very special thank you and lots of love. You did everything you could to help. To my parents, to Michael's mother, to our brothers and sisters, and to our many wonderful friends, I give my heartfelt thanks.

In addition I would like to express my deep appreciation for the work of several specialists whose expert medical care made a difference when the odds were all wrong, and also for the continuing care and assistance of our family physician. In the same way, I would like to thank the many nurses and other hospital staff who gave more than was required, who helped make the hospital a more pleasant place.

And also very special thanks to Kathy, to Jill, to Janet, to my father, my mother, and Eryn, for your helpful critiques of this manuscript.